"Are you just a ruthless businessman with his eye on the money to be made? Or do you have some real passion for what you do?"

It was issued as a challenge. That alone had knocked Adam further off balance. A few minutes ago she was trembling in his arms, and now she was standing toe-to-toe with him, as if they were in a fight for their lives.

"I admit that the house has a lot of potential, so much so that I couldn't wait to get my hands on it. But I want it for myself."

An elegant brow arched as she glared at him, and heat raced to Adam's groin. "Selfish aren't we?" she said.

He shrugged. "More like greedy." He took a step closer to her. "You see, Camille, when I see something I want, I stop at nothing to obtain it. And once I have it, it's mine until I'm ready to let it go."

To her credit, she didn't flinch, and Adam grew even more aroused. "That's a habit I'm sure you can stand to break, Adam," she said.

Books by A.C. Arthur

Kimani Romance

Love Me Like No Other
A Cinderella Affair

ARTIST C. ARTHUR

was born and raised in Baltimore, Maryland, where she currently resides with her husband and three children. An active imagination and a love of reading encouraged her to begin writing in high school, and she hasn't stopped since.

Determined to bring a new edge to romance, she continues to develop intriguing plots, racy characters and fresh dialogue—thus keeping readers on their toes! Visit her Web site at www.acarthur.net.

A
Cinderella
AFFAIR

A.C. ARTHUR

KIMANI
ROMANCE

KIMANI PRESS™

ISBN-13: 978-0-373-86031-9
ISBN-10: 0-373-86031-5

A CINDERELLA AFFAIR

www.kimanipress.com

Printed in U.S.A.

Dear Reader,

The Donovan men are back! This time it's Adam who's finding it hard to stick with their rule of never marrying.

A Cinderella Affair introduces Adam Donovan, one of the "Triple Threat" Donovans—known for their breathtaking good looks, the size of their bank accounts and their inability to commit to a lasting relationship. Only, Adam has something the newspapers never report about: compassion and integrity. It's Adam's big heart that has him falling hard and fast for Camille Davis.

Camille is so perfect for Adam and, surprisingly, it doesn't take him long to figure that out. The challenge for Adam is convincing Camille. Camille must overcome some very real obstacles before accepting Adam into her life, and I enjoyed watching her grow.

When you get a chance, please visit my Web site at www.acarthur.net for a closer look at the Donovan clan. And don't hesitate to share your comments about Linc and Jade via e-mail at acarthur22@yahoo.com.

A. C. Arthur

To fairy tales and happy endings.
I would be lost without them.

Chapter 1

Camille Davis swung the door open with so much force the knob slammed against the wall with a bang and the three people sitting at the conference table looked up instantly.

Out of breath from running down the hall to get to the designated conference room before this bogus deal could go any further, she stood there for a moment, chest heaving, suddenly unsure of what exactly she wanted to say.

"What are you doing here?" her stepmother asked as she stood, tossing her a more than disdainful look.

As Camille's heart rate slowed her anger grew. Moreen Scott Davis, her father's second wife, was impeccably dressed in a dark blue suit with silk lapels. Her glossy black hair framed her flawlessly made-up face. She looked like the twenty-first-century version of Diahann Carroll. Too bad she had a long way to go to ever be that classy.

"I should be asking you the same question," Camille said, taking a step closer to the table. There were two men gaping with surprise from her to Moreen but she wasn't concerned with them at the moment. Right now her top priority was nipping the Merry Widow in the bud. A task she'd been unhappily executing for the last three months.

That's when her father had died.

Randolph Davis, multimillionaire, A-list Hollywood producer, Moreen's third husband and Camille's beloved father, died of coronary disease in Cedars-Sinai Hospital one rainy July night at nine forty-five.

Camille was ten years old when Moreen, the tall, sexy model, had come into her room on her father's arm being introduced as her new stepmother. Camille had hid her fury initially, waiting until she'd had her father alone to explode. Even then Randolph had an uncanny way of calming her down. She'd been thoroughly upset at the thought of her father with another woman but then he'd explained things to her in a way that had her thinking only of his happiness. Camille loved her father too much to ever do anything that would make him unhappy.

She only wished his new wife had felt the same way. From day one Moreen made a point of informing Camille that decisions where she, the child, was concerned could no longer be manipulated through Randolph. That would now be Moreen's job. Private schools, summer camps and endless classes on etiquette and grooming were Moreen's idea of the perfect childhood. They were Camille's idea of torture.

Camille's mother had died when she was eight, from complications of pneumonia, her father said. And for two years Camille and her father had been close, relying only on each other to survive the darkest time in their lives. The darkest time, that is, until Moreen came. Her father was completely brainwashed by the sexy vixen.

Camille hated her.

That harsh emotion spun from the brash and uncaring way Moreen had of reminding Camille that she was *not* her child and that she was not worthy of all her father had showered on her. Remarks like, "I don't know why we waste money sending you to etiquette class, you'll never amount to anything," "You're so plain, so unattractive," "You're too short and too pudgy," had been the norm in the Davis household.

As a result, Camille struggled with depression and roller-coaster weight loss and gain. Finally, when she was in her second year of college Camille had collapsed. She was exhausted from working as an assistant in a design house and taking a full class load, and she was malnourished from trying to be like the skinny models she worked with on a daily basis. In essence, she was slowly killing herself.

Finally, when Camille had felt as if she were at the end of her rope, she'd decided to try seeing a counselor. That was her saving grace. Her counseling sessions were private, a place where she could share her innermost feelings without fear of her father finding out and having to face his rage at her exposing what he would have termed "private matters." She told of Moreen's verbal abuse and was rewarded by the fact that she was not the cause of her extremely low self-esteem, Moreen was. But even finding the cause didn't always heal the wound.

Now she was in a face-off with Moreen yet again. Only this time Camille planned to come out on top.

"I'm taking care of business," Moreen huffed.

"You're trying to sell my father's house without my permission."

"I don't need your permission."

"I own half of that house." Camille took another step closer to Moreen and tried not to flinch at the heated waves of animosity emanating from the woman to her. "You can't do anything with that house without my approval and my signature."

Then, as if she finally decided to acknowledge the two men still sitting at the table, Camille looked in their direction and asked, "Did you know that I owned half the house? Did you know that what you're trying to do here is illegal? Do you know that I can sue the pants off you and your big brass corporation for attempting to fraudulently buy my property?"

Her heart was pounding again and she didn't wait for their answer as she swung back to Moreen. "I don't know what it's going to take for you to get through your head that he left everything…down to his socks…to you and I. Fifty, fifty. Now I have no idea why he'd do such a fool thing but I am attempting to deal with that. You, on the other hand, seem to think you can do whatever it is you please no questions asked."

"Now you just wait a minute, young lady." Moreen stepped away from the table to get closer to Camille. "I don't know what's come over you—"

That made two of them because Camille didn't have a clue where she'd gotten the nerve to jump on a plane to Las Vegas, bumrush a major corporation and interrupt a meeting she was sure was worth millions of dollars. But at the present time none of that was relevant. The only thing that mattered was saving the house she'd grown up in, the house her mother had lived in.

She'd found out that Moreen was attempting to sell the house from her best friend and business partner, Dana Palmer, whose mother ran in the same social circles as Moreen. And she'd dropped everything to get here in time to stop her.

"I'm tired of dealing with your drama. Your father catered to you but I certainly will not."

"Ah, it seems that you two have some sort of personal issue going on here. But we were in the middle of a meeting and—" a male voice interrupted.

Camille paused, almost stopped breathing as she listened.

It couldn't be.

She'd dreamt of that voice.

Every night for the last six months, except for the two weeks after her father's death, she'd dreamt of that voice, that man.

The deep timbre resonated throughout her entire body. The sound moved from her ears and slithered down her spine spreading familiar spikes of warmth in its wake.

Camille paused, then moved in a way that had her convinced the entire room had been switched to slow motion.

Their gazes met and held.

"—ah, we were…" The man in her dreams cleared his throat.

It *was* him. From the close-cropped hair and smiling eyes to the strong jaw and not-too-thick lips. It was him and she didn't know how to react.

The man sitting beside her dream man stood. "What my partner is trying to say is that you and Mrs. Davis should probably deal with your family business at another time. We are in the middle of a very important meeting."

Moreen interrupted. "I must apologize. This is my stepdaughter, Camille Davis."

The man extended his hand and nodded. "I'm Maxwell Donovan."

Camille accepted his hand with a brief nod. He was certainly easy on the eyes with his caramel-toned skin and funny-colored eyes. But he was nothing in comparison to the man beside him. The man she couldn't bring herself to look at again.

"This is my partner, Adam Donovan."

Camille sighed. The man in her dreams now had a name.

It would be rude not to look at him now especially since he was also standing and extending his hand. She took a deep breath and accepted his hand as well.

In her more fanciful thoughts she expected sparks to fly or maybe fireworks to explode in the distant sky at their first touch. What she didn't expect was that warmth his voice had solicited to swirl and center in the pit of her stomach then slowly slither lower.

"It's a pleasure to meet you, Ms. Davis. Since you obviously have an interest in this deal, why don't you take a seat and join us," he said in that voice that Camille swore would make any woman scream.

Camille sat, ignoring Moreen's evil glare from beside her.

"As I was saying," Max continued. "This meeting was simply to get an idea of what was on the table. We haven't made any formal offers nor has Mrs. Davis accepted anything from us. However, we have done some preliminary investigation into the property. The property is a value all by itself. And the house, while in good condition, can be worth almost double once we're finished with it. Your father was a businessman—I'm sure you would agree that he would at least entertain our offer."

"It's too much space for me, Camille. And you haven't lived there in years," Moreen pleaded.

"It was my father's house. I was born there and I grew up there. It's not for sale," she said adamantly. "If she informed you otherwise then she was out of line."

Camille stood to leave. In her mind there was nothing more to discuss.

She expected the silence. Or maybe she expected Moreen to start on one of her tirades. What she did not expect—but probably should have since this seemed to be the year of surprises for her—was the touch on her arm.

"Why don't you hear us out and then decide if you're interested?" Adam asked.

Adam already knew he was interested...in her, that is.

The moment she walked in that door, he'd remembered. He'd sat in his seat and replayed the night he'd first met her.

His brother Linc had just gotten married, effectively disrupting the reputation of the Triple Threat Brothers. That's what Adam and his two older brothers were known as because of their good looks, hefty bank accounts and irrefutable desire to remain bachelors. Now the three were down to two, but Adam wasn't complaining. Linc had made a wise choice. Jade was a good woman and she made his brother a better man.

The wedding reception had gone into the early morning hours, long after the bride and groom had left for their honeymoon. Adam had been ready to leave.

Then he'd bumped into her.

She smelled of chic, expensive perfume and felt like silk the brief moment she was in his arms. He distinctly remembered looking down into her pixielike face, falling into deep chocolate-brown eyes, slightly slanted with a soulful depth that reached inside and clutched his heart instantly. Those eyes held secrets, pain and a longing he could almost identify with, and yet he didn't even know her name.

"Sorry." She spoke and the smoky sound of her voice slid through him with a slow and steady warmth, like fine wine.

He hadn't released his hold on her, although she was perfectly secure in standing on her own. He just couldn't bring himself to end the connection. She wore short sleeves and the soft skin beneath his hands was simply too tempting.

"Don't be. It was my fault. I should have looked where I was going," he'd said because he should say something. After all, staring was rude.

She made a move to leave and he panicked. "Wait! I mean, ah, are you staying at the hotel or just visiting?"

Tilting her head to the side made her hair—silky brown strands stopping abruptly at her chin—swish to one side, covering half of one eye. She stared at him and the low hum of attraction vibrated in his groin. She was shockingly sexy. Why that was a shock he couldn't quite put his finger on.

"I was in the casino and now I'm trying to leave. Is that okay with you?"

There was a definite bite to her words but the sarcasm didn't reach her eyes. He focused there because if his gaze dropped down to her lips again he'd most certainly have to kiss her. Then as if a lightbulb had gone off in his head he'd remembered who and where he was and released her. "Of course, it's okay. It's getting late—I just wanted to know if I needed to call you a cab or not."

She blinked, curiosity brimming in those alluring eyes. "No, thank you. I think I'll be fine."

She did move around him then, and when he'd turned was walking away with quick, purposeful strides. She wore slacks, nice, dark slacks designed most likely for comfort or businesslike attire that mysteriously aroused him.

He'd sighed and returned to the ballroom to

enjoy the festivities. And while she was gone from sight her presence still occupied space in his mind, so much so that sleep had been hard to come by.

He hadn't forgotten her but he hadn't expected to ever see her again, either.

Now she was here, standing in the conference room of Donovan Investments, Inc., throwing a very attractive monkey wrench in one of his biggest acquisitions.

She was the same and yet she was different. Her hair was swept up into a curly style that gave her an air of sophistication that didn't quite fit her. She was tense and guarded; agitated and uncertain. And he wanted to know why.

"I'm not interested," she said.

And he felt a slap to his ego. He had to remind himself that she wasn't telling him she was not interested in him personally. Still, her words stung.

"Just hear us out."

She sighed heavily and walked back to the table. Over her shoulder Adam caught a glimpse of Max's approving expression and suppressed a grin.

Donovan Investments, Inc. was growing steadily. He and Max were renowned for their sound investments and profitable turnarounds. It all began with a vacation in Bermuda three years ago. He'd ventured away from the resort where he was staying, walking along enjoying the view when he'd seen it. On a hill, almost hidden by trees, twin towers of beauty. Upon closer inspection he'd noted that beauty most definitely was in the eye of the beholder since the building was empty and almost in ruins. But Adam sensed the possibilities and bought it. His brothers were livid and about to harass him into getting rid of the dilapidated property but Max had come to his rescue. He'd flown to Bermuda and shared in Adam's vision. They renovated the hotel and sold it for twice what Adam had paid for it.

From that moment on they'd made one lucrative deal after another. Adam was a very rich man, although he would have been rich without Donovan Investments. But earning his own money seemed so much more appealing to Adam than just living off what was his solely by birthright.

"It really makes sense to go ahead and sell, Camille," Moreen said.

Adam looked at the older woman. This was his first time meeting her in person. Max had taken care of the initial phone calls and scheduled this meeting. Adam sensed a lot of hostility between the two women. As much as he didn't want to get involved in any family feud he couldn't help but feel like Camille needed someone on her side.

"You took my father away from me. Is it really imperative for you to take everything?" Camille asked.

"What are your intentions for the house?" Adam interrupted. He'd heard the sincerity in her words and the pain. Randolph Davis had died three months ago, three months after the first time he'd seen her. He remembered the look of discontent in her eyes that night in the casino and couldn't help but notice that it was magnified now.

And then she looked at him and Adam felt as if he were sinking, falling into those deep brown eyes, into her pain and despair. A part of him hurt for her and he suppressed the urge to go to her and hold her.

Adam had always been the more caring of the Donovan men, the compassionate one who had a soft spot for the ladies. Once upon a time that soft spot had garnered him a broken heart. Kim Alvarez was her name. She was his college sweetheart, the woman he'd been ready to spend the rest of his life with, until fate had stepped in and shown him the error of his ways.

And while Adam had sworn never to take that route again he didn't miss the opportunity to help a damsel in distress when he saw one. Somehow he knew that Camille's distress was unlike any other he'd ever experienced.

"I…I don't know," she stammered.

"Exactly," Moreen continued quickly. "That's why we need to go ahead with this deal now. Camille, they aren't going to wait forever for you to make up your mind."

"My mind is already made up," Camille retorted.

Adam looked at Max who appeared to be at the end of his rope with this meeting. "Okay, why don't we do this. Mrs. Davis has a room at the Gramercy, right?"

Moreen nodded. "Yes. I do."

"Great. Then if Ms. Davis does not have a room I'm sure we can get you one since my brother owns the hotel." Adam smiled because he desperately wanted Camille to smile, too, and because he hoped his mention of the hotel reminded her of the night they first met. "Then we can meet again tomorrow morning after everybody's had the chance to digest these new developments."

"I already have a plane ticket to go back to L.A. tonight," Camille said.

She had the prettiest complexion, like a cup of hot chocolate, and the way she stared up at him made her look even more vulnerable. Not caring how out of place it was or that Max would definitely have something to say about it later, Adam got up from his seat and walked around to the other side of the table. He knelt down next to the chair she sat in and took her hand. "Why don't you and I have some dinner and discuss what it is you have in mind for your father's estate. I'll share what Donovan Investments is offering and then you can decide. If you're still not interested I'll take you to the airport."

She seemed to be thinking it over. He however, was loving the feel of her smooth skin beneath his touch. She smelled sweet and alluring, just as she had before. This was a big deal for him and the company and Adam had a strange feeling that Camille wasn't going to easily be convinced to sell the property. He hated to admit that at this moment that wasn't his top priority. Spending more time with her was.

"I don't want to sell," she said quietly.

"Just give me a chance to talk to you," he implored.

Then as if she knew he'd been holding his breath waiting for that very action, she smiled. His insides warmed and the voice of dread echoed in the back of his mind.

This was so unlike her. Camille did not date often and when she did it was with men she'd met on more than one occasion. However, tonight she found herself sitting in the only restaurant on the ground floor of the Gramercy Hotel with the man who had haunted her dreams for months. She'd already missed her flight back to L.A. so it was agreed that she was staying in Vegas.

She'd remembered the weekend she'd spent here. The weekend she'd been Dana's maid of honor and had been forced to do her bidding. Well, she couldn't exactly call it being forced.

Dana Palmer was Camille's best friend and had been since the summer Camille turned eleven—the summer after her father had married Moreen. A soft smile touched her lips as she remembered the impromptu slumber parties on those nights when

Moreen was just too much to stand and through each of her bad relationships. Dana had provided that sense of balance Camille needed. When Moreen would verbally attack her, stripping her of all self-confidence and self-esteem, Dana would attempt to build her right back up.

Camille would do anything for Dana. Almost anything.

"This is your weekend. For three days it is my job to do whatever I can to make you happy," Camille remembered saying. It was at that precise moment that he'd walked in.

The same man she'd bumped into on her way to meet Dana. This was Camille's first trip to Vegas and her first time in a real live casino. She had no idea that casinos were hotels as well as money pits.

He'd been extremely attractive and he'd made her nervous. She was happy to get away from him, yet sad that she hadn't had enough courage to talk to him like a sane adult woman.

"I want you to sleep with him," Dana had said as she took another sip from her drink.

Camille had followed her gaze and immediately began shaking her head negatively.

"Uh-huh. You are out of your mind." She had immediately turned her back to the "him" Dana had been referring to, her hands already beginning to sweat.

"Come on, Camille, he looks positively yummy!" Dana had squealed.

"Then you do him," Camille had shot back while reaching for her drink. She'd gripped the glass, brought it to her lips, then decided she needed something much stronger. "Rum and Coke, please," she'd asked the bartender who thankfully appeared just in time.

"I'm about to be a married woman, I can't do him. But you're single, so you should go for it."

Camille had tossed Dana a disgusted look. "I am happily single and couldn't manage to 'do him' if I tried."

"What are you thinking about over there?"

His voice startled her from her memories and Camille jumped in her seat. She'd been so caught up in her thoughts that she'd forgotten she was now sitting across from the man she'd refused to "do" almost six months ago.

"What? Oh, I'm sorry. What were you saying?" She picked up her napkin and placed it in her lap. She needed something to do with her hands to keep them from shaking. Dating wasn't something Camille proclaimed to do well. And that was mostly because she was self-conscious about her looks.

Taking a deep breath, Camille reminded herself that this was not a date. And that while Adam Donovan was her sexy dream guy, she was in no way the subject of his dreams. This was business to him. Business, she reminded herself, was something she could definitely do.

"I noticed. You were pretty deep in thought. Do you want to share?" he asked.

He looked at her quizzically, not disapprovingly, she quickly noted. "No. It was nothing." She cleared her throat. "I'd rather talk about you. I mean, I'd rather talk about your plans for my father's house and why you approached only one of the owners."

Their food arrived so conversation was stalled for a few minutes. Adam had ordered the Porterhouse steak and roasted potatoes with steamed asparagus. Camille's stomach lurched as the waiter put a huge salad in front of her. She attempted to focus on her salad, sprinkling it with lemon juice instead of salad dressing.

Adam took a bite and moaned. "Linc has got the best chef in town. I swear I've been to just about all of the upscale restaurants in Vegas and have never experienced a steak so tender and seasoned as this one."

Camille stifled a moan of her own and stuffed a forkful of lettuce and croutons into her mouth. When Adam looked to her for a response she simply smiled and nodded.

"Is that all you're going to eat?" he asked as he cut another piece of steak.

She nodded. "Yes, I'm not that hungry." That was a blatant lie and if he could only hear the revolting sounds her stomach was making he'd know that.

"I never could understand how rabbit food could

fill a human stomach. My mother serves a salad with every meal. Made me want to puke when I was growing up."

Camille smiled and tilted her head to stare at him. "I'll bet you were an obedient child," she said absently.

"And you'd lose every dime of your money." He chuckled. "My mother could tell you stories of how mischievous I was. One time when my cousins were at the house I convinced them and my brothers to take the mattress off our beds and slide down the grand staircase in the foyer." He laughed loudly then. "We had the best time."

Camille laughed with him because his smile reached his eyes which held hers captive. She laughed because the deep, sincere sound of his enjoyment touched a spot in her that she was sure she'd lost long ago. "What did your parents do?"

"Mom blistered my butt something terrible. But that was nothing new. Out of my three brothers I got in the most trouble."

Camille stopped eating, placing her elbows on the table. Then as if she were right at the table with them, Camille heard Moreen's shrill voice chastising her, "Take your elbows off the table." Abruptly she pulled her arms down and dropped her hands in her lap. She prayed Adam hadn't noticed but the moment she looked up she knew he had.

"Ah, are you older than your brothers?" she asked quietly.

Adam took a sip of his wine. "I am the youngest of the three and I'm twenty-nine."

"I don't have any brothers or sisters."

"That must have been pretty lonely for you growing up, huh?"

"Yes, it was." She found herself about to tell him how lonely and how painful her childhood had been but then she remembered this was not a social evening. She sat up straighter in the chair and resumed the pretense of enjoying her salad. "So you didn't tell me why you thought you could buy a property with only one owner's consent. You and your brother don't strike me as simple-minded businessmen."

He almost choked on his food and Camille quickly lifted his glass of water and handed it to him.

He nodded and took the glass from her. "Thank you," he murmured. He took a gulp then set the glass down. "You are correct. My brother and I are not simple-minded. This deal came up kind of sudden. I assumed that Max had taken care of the legwork, which I am sure he did. Details must have gotten misconstrued somehow."

"Yes, the tiny detail of my name beside hers on the will. Misconstruing details is right up Moreen's alley," she said dryly.

"You don't like your stepmother much, do you?"

"Does it show?"

Adam chuckled and held his two fingers together. "Just a tiny bit."

Camille smiled again. Adam Donovan had a way of making her smile. That was something she wasn't used to with a man. Actually, she wasn't sure she'd smiled at all in the past six months.

"But now that we know there are two owners, we will approach the deal accordingly. Donovan Investments has no desire to cause a family feud or to face any legal hassles."

"Good. Then you can tell your brother that there is nothing to approach. I don't want to sell my father's house."

"So you plan on moving into it?"

"No. I have a condo in the city. It's close to my shop and it's my own personal space. I need my personal space."

Adam nodded. "I know what you mean. Our house was big but it was always filled with people. So I couldn't wait to get a place of my own where I could stretch out and do my own thing."

She didn't respond. She didn't want to talk about personal things with him anymore.

"So what kind of shop do you have?" he asked.

"Ah, it's a design shop. I'm a fashion designer."

Adam contemplated her words. "*You're* CK Davis Designs?" he asked incredulously.

Camille slammed her fork down then took a deep breath trying to control her wayward emotions. "Don't sound so surprised." She couldn't help feeling a bit hurt by his question. As if she, the ranting woman that had interrupted their big meeting, couldn't possibly be capable of owning a business.

"I wasn't in any way insulting you. I own several of your suits and my mother loves your stuff. I'm just amazed that I'm actually sitting here with you."

That's it, she was a goner. Camille's heart fluttered and turned somersaults at his words. *He* was flattered to be here with *her.* She could just picture him in a CK Davis suit. The head of her men's department was Palio Victor, a very talented man who obviously knew what other men were looking for in clothes.

Here she was having dinner with a notoriously handsome man who had just admitted to being happy to be with her. If she were naïve enough to believe that she could have that type of luck she'd be ecstatic at the possibilities presenting themselves. But she knew better.

Adam Donovan was happy to be with her for one reason and one reason only, her father's house.

This was business to him. She was just a way to get the deal he wanted.

It wasn't personal. He wasn't really sitting here with Camille, the woman. Why would a man as rich and good-looking as he was ever want to do that?

Adam watched her closely. There was something about the way she looked. She had very expressive eyes, ones that gave away each and every emotion she felt at the exact time she was feeling it.

He'd watched her go from simmering anger to eager curiosity to extreme sadness. And with each change his need to know her better increased.

Now, he watched the way her gaze flitted around the room, to see if anyone was watching them, he presumed. He rarely gave consideration to other people or what they said about him. As one of the Triple Threat Brothers he was always in one newspaper or another. Whether it be about his business or what the press assumed was going on in his personal life, he and his brothers had garnered their share of front-page appearances. He'd learned long ago to take it all in stride.

Adam sat back in his chair and gave this situation as much serious thought as he could muster at the moment. His carefree persona did not allow him to overly examine situations like this. The one thing he knew for certain was that he liked Camille Davis.

He'd watched her back at the office as that conference room had cleared. She was graceful and elegant, yet still a bit timid. He hadn't tried to touch her as he'd so desperately wanted to, but instead had led her out of the room and to his waiting car in front of the building. She'd sat close to the door as if she planned to throw herself out of the car if he made one false move.

And a lot of moves had crossed his mind. Her perfume was soft and delicate and floated through the interior of the car, casting him under a heady sensual spell. His blood pumped hard and fast throughout his body, desire building a wall of tension at the base of his neck as he sensed this would not be an easy conquest. Some women took more time, more finesse than others. Camille Davis was one of those women.

"Your father was a good man," he said because she was looking like she was about to take off at any moment. That confused him a bit. She seemed to have a very contradictory personality. She'd barged into that meeting this afternoon with confidence and spunk but now that she was here, alone with him, she seemed tense and withdrawn. "I met him once about a year ago. That's when I first got the idea to buy his house."

Her eyes focused on him. "You asked my father if you could buy the house? What did he say?"

"It was a very impromptu meeting. I was in L.A. I'd seen a picture of the house in a magazine at a hotel. I was so impressed by the photos I showed up on his doorstep. And because he recognized my name he let me in. He was very gracious and gave me a grand tour. I asked what the price tag was and he laughed." Adam smiled as he remembered that evening. "He offered me a drink and told me that houses were for sale but his home was his sanctuary and there weren't enough zeroes in the balance of the Federal Reserve that would make him part with it."

She nodded. "That sounds like something Daddy would say."

There it was, that tiny spark in her eyes, that wistful bit of happiness that she refused to take hold of. He wondered why she was so intent on being sad. "I don't want you to think I'm a vulture. I did not pounce on this property the moment I heard your father had passed." Her opinion of him was important. Why, he wasn't quite sure.

"If you know that he didn't want to sell it while he was living why are you trying to get it now?"

He sighed because her gaze pierced him. She was making him think about this deal way too deeply. "Because it's my business. It's what I do."

"You buy properties that aren't for sale?" she inquired while slowly lifting her glass to her lips.

He didn't miss the bite in her words and found he preferred even that to her looking sad and defeated. "I find properties with the potential to make me a lot of money. I buy them and I renovate them. Then I resell them for a profit."

"A shrewd business man, I see."

Adam shrugged. "I'm good at it."

"I'm good at cursing people out but I don't do it for a living," she snapped.

He smiled. "I'm not a hitman or a traitor. I'm an investor. It's a legitimate business, not to mention a profitable one. It's sort of like you being a designer."

She frowned. "How do you figure that?"

"You look at old styles, old clothes that used to work or used to be in fashion. And then you put a new spin on them. You add more expensive material and your classic level of design." He smiled because he could see that she was seeing the similarities. "And then you sell them, making yourself a tidy profit."

She dropped her fork and glared at him. "Whatever. I am not selling my father's house and this dinner is over."

She was pushing her chair back, about to stand, when he reached across the table and grabbed her wrist. It was an impulsive move. He didn't know why he'd done it and he didn't know what he planned to do now that he had. All he knew for certain was that the thought of her walking out of the restaurant and out of his life again was too much to bear.

She stilled. He loosened his grip, letting his fingers rest complacently. He noted the erratic thumping of her pulse and wondered briefly if she were afraid of him. If so, he definitely wasn't winning any brownie points. He took a deep breath and tried to regroup.

Women loved his smile. They said it made him seem more human, more approachable than his brothers. So he smiled.

She arched an eyebrow. "You can either let my arm go or I can scream for security. Which do you prefer?"

He pulled his hand away as if he'd been burned and watched in amazement as she stood. Never once in all his years of wooing women had his signature smile not worked.

Then, because she was about to walk away, he hurriedly stood and moved in front of her, being careful not to touch her this time. "I thought we were going to talk about the house. You haven't even heard why I want to buy it."

Camille rolled her eyes and folded her arms over her chest, an action that lifted her heavy breasts upward until he could see even more of the creamy mounds above the rim of her blouse. Adam swallowed. Hard.

"You said you buy houses and then sell them. That's your job so I assume that's what you plan to do with my father's house. If so, I am not interested."

Damn, she was sexy when she was angry. Adam had visions of having a knock down, drag out argument with her then scooping her up into his arms and releasing all that frustration in the bedroom. She would let loose then, he knew it instinctively. She would be uninhibited, passionate and seductive. His head pounded as the blood rushed from there to his groin. She would be magnificent.

"Are you not interested because you dislike me or because you dislike your stepmother?"

She gasped as if he'd struck her and took a step back.

He instinctively reached for her, catching her elbow before she could pull away. "Camille, I'm just trying to have an intelligent conversation about this deal with you. In all fairness you really haven't given a valid reason for not wanting this deal to go through."

"It's *my* property. I don't have to have a valid reason," she taunted.

Adam sighed. He never worked this hard to get a woman into bed. He'd never had to. That probably made him callous and arrogant where women were concerned and up until now he hadn't given that a second thought. But he readily admitted that Camille Davis was beginning to try his patience.

"Why don't you tell me why you really want to hold on to this house. You have no intention of living there, so what—do you want it to be like some sort of shrine to your father's memory?"

She did pull away from him then. "You don't know anything about me or my father. You're just used to getting your way. Well, it's not going to happen this time."

Before Adam could say another word he was watching the enticing sway of her hips as she walked out of the restaurant. Damn, that woman infuriated him. And made him hard as hell.

Chapter 2

"So who is she?" Trenton Donovan asked gruffly.

Adam shifted on the couch. They were in his oldest brother, Linc's office, on the top floor of the Gramercy Casino. Max had obviously called this little meeting and so was sitting in one of the deep leather chairs across the room while Trent stood near the window, his hands thrust into his pockets as he glared at Adam. Linc was sitting behind his desk being uncharacteristically quiet. But then, Adam sighed, he'd only been in here for about five minutes.

After being left standing like a fool in the middle of the restaurant Adam had ditched the idea of returning to his condo on the outskirts of Vegas and decided to get a room at the hotel. Of course he had no difficulty getting one and as he'd retrieved his key from the clerk at the front desk he'd also received a message to come to Linc's office immediately.

So that's why he was here. Not by any choice of his own because if he had his choice he'd have been in a nice comfy room with a big bed and a beautiful, if high-strung, woman.

With that thought he frowned oblivious to his audience's extreme pleasure.

"Wow, she's that bad, huh?" Max asked. "So where does the deal stand?"

Adam dragged a hand down his face and attempted a casual response. "She's not that bad and the deal isn't dead." He had no idea why he'd said that. It was a blatant contradiction to what Camille had told him just before walking away.

"She changed her mind?"

"Who is she?"

Trent and Max spoke simultaneously and Linc chuckled. "Give him a second to get his bearings, guys. He looks like he's had a pretty eventful dinner."

Normally Adam and Max tended to side against the two older Donovans. Tonight it seemed that all three of them were against him. He didn't miss the unspoken words that had the other Donovan men watching him carefully. "What's up? She's Randolph Davis's daughter just like she said. And she's not entirely sold on the idea of getting rid of her father's house. But I plan to change her mind," he said decisively.

It was Max's turn to frown this time. "How do you plan to do that? She looked quite decided when she left the conference room. I don't know why you even offered to put her up for the night. Meeting with her again tomorrow is most likely not going to change anything."

Adam swore and the three pair of eyes that were already watching him closely moved in on him.

"We're not meeting with her tomorrow?" Max asked.

"Yes. We are." Adam stood. He hadn't gotten around to setting a time and place for tomorrow because he'd been so into the simple conversation he and Camille were having. She'd been the one to bring up business and she'd been the one to end their evening. He hadn't been given much of an opportunity to say anything and at this moment that was really pissing him off.

"Camille Davis. Her name sounds familiar," Linc said as he leaned back in his chair and rubbed his chin.

"You may have heard of her company, CK Davis Designs," Adam said absently. He went to the small bar on the other side of the office and fixed himself a drink. His mind whirled with all the things he hadn't had a chance to say to Camille. He'd already decided he was going to say his piece, and since he was putting her up in this hotel for the night, she was going to go through with their meeting tomorrow. She wouldn't be happy to hear that but he didn't rightfully care. This was business. He should never have let the personal interfere, no matter how desirable and totally kissable she appeared.

"She's *the* C.K. Davis? That's a multi-million-dollar company. Her stocks are through the roof and the winter line she's debuting in a couple of weeks is reputed to be her best yet. She's a definite powerhouse in the fashion industry." Max had stood and was now pacing the floor. "She'll never sell that house. She doesn't need the money so there's no reason for her to sell. At least the stepmother is greedy so we have something to work with there, but the daughter is going to be trouble."

"Calm down, Max." Adam took a long swallow of his brandy. "I'm going to close this deal."

"If she's a designer and she's rich I could probably dig up some dirt on her. That'll make her cooperate."

Adam tossed Trent a searing look. "Don't you dare! Your secret security skills are not required in this instance." Trent always wanted to investigate somebody. He was an ex-Navy Seal and therefore tended to look at every situation as if it were a military deployment.

Trent shrugged. "I'm just trying to help."

"Investigating someone's personal life is not helping," Adam argued.

"Funny, you didn't always feel that way," Linc added.

Adam sighed. "That was different. You were sleeping with Jade and she was staying in our parents' house. We had a right to know everything about her."

Linc stood. "No. I had a right to know everything about her, not you."

Max interrupted. "For crying out loud, you and Jade are happily married. Can we please try to focus on the matter at hand?"

Adam turned to Max. "*We* could focus on our business matters if you hadn't brought *them* into the mix. You know how they are."

"Hey, we're family," Linc objected. "Whether or not we're all in the same business doesn't matter. If one needs help that's what the rest of us are here for."

"But I don't need any help," Adam insisted.

Linc crossed the room and placed a hand on his brother's shoulder. "If you're going to try and convince a woman to change her mind you're going to need all the help you can get."

"I usually don't have any problems where women are concerned," Adam said absently.

Linc grinned. "Then that tells me that this is an unusual woman. In which case you might need more than our help."

* * *

Adam didn't need anything but to see Camille Davis one more time.

Not in that way, he convinced himself.

He only wanted to tell her about the meeting tomorrow. At least that was the reason he'd taken the elevator to the tenth floor instead of the fifteenth where his room was.

He knocked on the door determined to get this over with as quickly as possible. And then she answered.

"Hello."

Her voice seemed small now that they were face to face. In the restaurant there had been plenty of background noise so he'd had no problem hearing her. She still wore the slacks and blouse she had on earlier but she'd taken off the jacket. The chocolaty brown skin of her bare arms showed and he had to take a deep breath before speaking.

"Hi." To his own ears his voice didn't sound as confident as he would have liked so he looked over her shoulders for a momentary reprieve. "If you're not busy I need to speak with you for a moment."

Camille wasn't busy. In fact, she was just enjoying a minor pity party before he'd knocked. The moment she'd closed that door behind her an hour earlier she'd been hit with the biggest wave of disappointment she'd ever felt. She'd acted rude and selfishly to Adam Donovan, a man who had been nothing but nice to her since she'd crashed his meeting.

She'd plopped down onto the couch, unable to enjoy the luxurious room he'd secured for her because she couldn't get past the ill feelings towards his business deal and all that it stood for. He wanted to buy her father's house, to take away the last memory she'd ever have of what being loved felt like.

That was the reason she did not want to sell the house but she couldn't tell Adam Donovan that. He'd never understand. He had a great family who apparently loved him very much. He couldn't possibly relate to her holding on to a piece of property as a way of staying connected to her father.

She'd already resigned herself to apologizing to him but thought she would at least have until tomorrow morning when she'd managed to secure herself a new outfit and a good night's rest first. But he was here so there was no better time like the present.

"No. I'm not busy at all. Come on in." Stepping to the side she allowed him entrance and inhaled the scent of his cologne as he walked by. With an inward groan she berated herself for once more entertaining the silly notion that she could be attracted to a man like him.

"We didn't get a chance to talk about what time would be good for you to meet tomorrow," Adam began as soon as he was in the sitting area of her room.

"I know," she started to say then felt herself fidgeting and pushed her hands behind her back so he wouldn't glimpse her nervousness. "First, I should apologize for the way I left earlier. It was rude and unprofessional."

Adam looked shocked for a moment, then gave a half smile. "It's okay. I've been told I can be a bit pushy at times. I apologize if I offended you."

"Oh, no." Camille shook her head quickly. "You didn't offend me. I mean, I shouldn't have been offended by your questions. They were harmless. I just have a tendency to overreact sometimes."

"Really? So were you overreacting to having dinner with me or to the business we were discussing?"

With a small jerk of her arms Camille demanded her hands be still. She squared her shoulders and was determined to look him straight in the eye and answer him. Adam Donovan did not make her nervous. There was no need for her to be. He was here on business. But *here* was in a hotel room where just a few feet away was a huge elegantly adorned bed.

"I overreacted to your questions. At any rate, it's over now. What time do you want to meet?" Before he could answer she put a hand up to stop him. "Keep in mind that I am only agreeing to this meeting because it was too late for me to get a flight back to L.A. and that was a part of our bargain. I don't make a habit of going back on my word. It doesn't mean that I've changed my mind about the sale."

He took a step closer to her and Camille felt her lungs struggling to take in air. Behind her back her hands clutched again.

"You still haven't heard my plans for the house, Camille."

"It doesn't matter," she said, her voice shaky and unfamiliar. He was only a couple of inches away now and his scent drifted around her, cloaking her until she felt like she was securely surrounded. He was looking at her strangely, his eyes having darkened a bit since when he'd first arrived.

She took a step back.

"I've been known to be very persuasive," he said in a deep, sexy voice.

"I can't be persuaded," she breathed and took another step back.

He reached out then and grabbed her shoulders. "Never move backwards," he warned. "You'll eventually be cornered."

And that she was. Behind her was the couch; one more step back and she would have fallen down onto it and as close as Adam was he would have fallen down right on top of her. A position she had no intention of them being in.

She was gorgeous, in a quiet, sneak-up-and-bite-you kind of way. Her chin was strong, her body singing every love song in the book to any man lucky enough to be around her. Her lips were small but plump and very kissable. But it was her eyes that held him captive. With their exotic shape and mystical color Adam couldn't help but be swept away. So much so that he'd forgotten that this was supposed to be business and was touching her in a very personal way. She was small, almost a foot shorter than him. He could have easily picked her up and dropped her in the center of that bed he'd spied upon entering. But he found that pushing her to her limits was much more enjoyable.

He made her nervous; he could tell by the way her eyes watched him closely and her body shifted restlessly. He could ease that restlessness. He could nip the nervousness in the bud if she'd let him kiss her. There was a keen attraction sizzling between them and Adam was willing to bet she was feeling it, too. He wondered what would happen if he pushed a little more.

"What if we started with something a little simpler than the discussion about the house," he suggested, moving his hands up and down her bare arms, loving the feel of her smooth skin against his.

"What do you mean?" she stammered.

"I mean, what if we talked about something else. Something a little less serious." She hadn't pulled away from him, which was a good sign, but he suspected that would be kind of hard for her to do since her legs were blocked by both him and the couch.

"Adam." Her hands came up to his chest in a small form of protest.

Right through his shirt the heat from her touch

burned him until he wanted to rip away the material that posed as a barrier to feel her skin to skin.

She pushed slightly and Adam had to take a deep, steadying breath. Never before had he been this turned on by a woman and never before had his desire interfered with his business. So he counted to three then forcefully pulled his hands away from her. It took another moment or two before he could step away, but he did.

"There is nothing for us to discuss except for the house," she said.

Adam turned away from her then because to keep staring at her only fueled this growing need in the pit of his stomach. This fierce desire to have her, totally.

"I'm sure you realize how untrue that statement is, Camille," he said as he turned back to face her.

"No. I mean, I don't know what you're talking about."

She was fidgeting again, a trait he found strangely endearing. Normally he liked decisive, fun and easygoing women who were down for a good time. He made it a point to stay away from emotionally driven women with too many issues for him to count. So why was he so drawn to her? He'd known her less than twenty-four hours and yet he knew without a doubt that Camille Davis had issues. Funny thing was, he wanted to know what those issues were and he wanted to fix them.

He had to clench his teeth at that one because he

definitely did not understand what was going on. What he did know was that two grown adults were standing in this room and that they were attracted to each other. He wasn't about skirting around any issues like that, business or pleasure. "I'm talking about this thing between us. It's obvious that we're attracted to each other. So whether or not we go into business together we'll still have to deal with that."

Slowly she brought her hands from behind her back and folded her arms over her chest. If she had any idea how hard that one act made him she would never do it again. Adam didn't move a muscle.

"There is nothing between us but my father's house. Anything else is purely your imagination."

He chuckled. "You'd like to think that, wouldn't you? It makes you feel safer if you convince yourself that there is nothing else between us. What I don't understand is why you need to feel safe. Do I frighten you, Camille?"

Her chin instantly went up, her eyes glaring at him as her anger grew. Adam almost smiled. She had some feistiness in her and some passion, he'd seen that in her eyes when he was close to her. There was a lot more to Camille Davis than met the eye.

"You do not frighten me. That's absurd. This entire conversation is absurd." She huffed. "The only reason you and I are even in the same room speaking to one another is because you want something that I have."

That was a vast understatement, Adam thought with amusement.

She was pacing back and forth now. "I mean, I live in L.A. and you live in Vegas, Sin City. What happens in Vegas stays in Vegas," she ranted. "We are not the same types of people so it's totally insane to think that we'd be attracted to each other."

Adam watched her agile movements. He watched every curve of her body move in sync as she spoke. Her arms rotated between being folded at her chest to swaying fitfully at her waist. It was at those times that he glimpsed her perfectly round bottom and those high, enticing breasts. She talked as if she had a lot of things going through her mind at once and she was having trouble keeping them all straight. He sensed it was because she was in fact nervous and unwilling to admit to what he already knew.

She was just as amazed by this instant attraction as he was. Only he was used to physical awareness and sexual tension. He knew just how to deal with them both and boasted a gold medal in doing so. However, he had a sneaky suspicion Camille would not be impressed by that knowledge.

He had no choice but to touch her again; if not she would have worn a hole in the floor. Besides, he had no problem putting his hands on Camille and hoped to do it more often. But for right now he wanted to calm her down. She was working herself into a fine fit and he needed to nip it in the bud. He caught her waist on another one of her trips past him and pulled her back against his chest. Keeping one arm around her waist he braced the other around her arms to keep them still.

"Camille." He breathed her name into her hair and struggled to keep from doing more. "I am a man. And you are a woman. Everything else is inconsequential."

Camille's heart beat erratically. She'd been so surprised when he grabbed her that she'd clamped her mouth shut, almost biting off her own tongue. He was too close and he was holding her and she couldn't breathe. But then she could breathe, his scent, that smell that both teased and tortured her.

She felt a little faint and wondered what she'd eaten today besides the partial salad at dinner. She was light-headed because she hadn't eaten three meals like she was supposed to. That's probably why she was going off the deep end in front of this virtual stranger.

"Dammit, you're shaking," Adam said as he spun her around to face him. "What's wrong with you? And don't tell me nothing because I'm not going to believe it."

He was speaking loudly now. That deep voice that she'd initially thought was sexy was now too loud and causing a pounding in her head. "Stop," she said slowly. "Please let me go."

"No. I'm not going to let you go until you tell me what's wrong."

She shook her head. "Nothing. It's nothing. Maybe you should just leave. We'll talk tomorrow." She tried to pull away from him but she was really shaky and the next thing she knew he was scooping her up into his arms and carrying her to the couch.

He set her down gently and Camille closed her eyes in supreme embarrassment. Her insides were on fire and she felt the sweat beginning to prick her forehead. She thought she had these episodes under control. She hadn't been to therapy in two months because she'd felt okay with herself. Why was this happening now, in front of him?

"Baby, what can I do? Do you want me to call a doctor or something? Talk to me, Camille."

She sighed heavily. "I don't need a doctor."

"Okay. Then tell me what you need. Whatever it is I'll get it for you."

Camille opened her eyes and wanted desperately to tell him what it was she secretly longed for. She wanted to tell somebody, anybody who would listen to a young girl's foolish dream. She'd had that dream for so long it had become a part of her life. And while she knew it would never come true, it was comforting just to have it.

Adam Donovan and his warm brown eyes, his easy smile and even easier charm had made her think of that dream again. He'd made her think of all that she wanted and would never have.

"I just need to be alone, that's all." She turned away from him then, burying her face in the back of the couch, hoping like hell he'd think she was a waste of time and leave her there.

She wasn't prepared for the gentle touch to her cheek or the soft whisper coming from him. "I won't leave you like this. Even if you don't tell me what's wrong I'm going to stay until you're feeling better."

Camille turned back slowly to find his face only inches from hers. He smiled and she wanted to cry at his sweetness. Instead she chuckled nervously. "You must think I'm some type of lunatic. First, I walk out on you in the restaurant and now this. I'm such a mess."

Adam laughed with her but continued to stroke her cheek with his fingers. "You're definitely not an ordinary date. But I've seen stranger things happen."

"I don't date often," she blurted out, then watched as his eyes grew in surprise.

"Really? I would have guessed you had a string of boyfriends back in L.A."

She didn't know why she'd admitted that to him but couldn't take the words back so instead she answered, "No boyfriends."

"Since how long?"

She shrugged. "I don't know. I think I had a date for my last showing, which was earlier this year. But that was only the one night. I didn't see him again afterwards."

He looked at her quizzically. "Have you ever had a real boyfriend?"

Feeling a little steadier, Camille struggled to sit up. Adam accommodated her by moving back and lifting her legs onto his lap as he sat down. "I'm not a puritan," she said dismally. "I just don't have a lot of free time."

"That didn't answer my question," he said as he slipped off her shoes and began rubbing her feet.

Camille thought to protest then figured she would have to be out of her mind to stop sensations this good. "I had a boyfriend in college."

"College? That long ago, huh?"

"I told you I don't have a lot of time. I'm trying to get my company off the ground."

"Your company is doing great. I told you I had a few suits and my mother is a huge fan. My brothers were even talking about you earlier tonight."

His hands moved up to her calves and Camille almost moaned. "Your brothers? Why would your brothers be talking about me?"

"My family and I are very close. So close that sometimes I can't have a thought without them knowing it."

He looked a little stressed by this admission. "You sound as if that bothers you."

"Not really." He shrugged. "Well, sometimes I guess it does."

They grew silent and then his hands rested on her thighs. "Are you ready to tell me what happened now?"

Camille sighed. Her father used to do the same thing. He'd rock her and talk to her about nonsense and then he'd approach the problem. Why did that endear Adam Donovan to her more? "I have panic attacks sometimes. I get really worked up and then I have a meltdown. But I'm okay now."

Adam stared at her seriously. "You're not all right. You haven't had the meltdown yet."

Camille smiled then broke out into laughter as she watched his eyes lighten and his lips spread into a wide grin. "I guess you're right but that'll have to wait until I'm alone. I absolutely refuse to melt down in front of a stranger."

"Hey, I'm no stranger. I've fed you and massaged your feet. That has to make me more along the lines of a friend."

Camille grew silent. "I don't need a friend."

Adam cupped her chin in his palm. "But you do need something, Camille. If you stop denying it maybe you'll find it soon."

Camille sighed contentedly and rolled over, snuggling into the soft sheets. Her body felt rested, her mind clear as she dropped an arm over her forehead. Her internal body clock said it was time to get up so she looked to the nightstand to gauge the time. She was a habitual early riser, sometimes too early. Today, she vowed if it were one of those too-early mornings she was going to lie in this comfortable bed a little longer.

It was nine-thirty. Camille shot straight up in the bed in horror and looked at the clock again. Surely she wasn't seeing clearly. She never slept this late. But it was nine-thirty—in fact it was now nine thirty-three. Pushing back the sheets she scrambled off the bed and was about to make her way into the bathroom when she realized she wasn't at home.

The peach curtains and emerald-green carpet was a dead giveaway. She was a fan of more subtle colors and so her bedroom was decorated in shades of gray and navy. For a minute her heart beat rampantly, then memories of yesterday came flooding back and she calmed. She was in Las Vegas. She'd come here to stop Moreen from selling her father's home. And she'd seen her dream guy again.

She fell back on the bed remembering the way he looked in that suit, like a male model posing in a boardroom. He was gorgeous. Hell, he was beyond gorgeous, but then she'd known that the first night they'd bumped into each other. She'd also known he was not on her menu. That's why she had resigned herself to only dreaming about him.

But fate seemed to have another plan. Adam Donovan was no longer only in her dreams. He was now officially a thorn in her side. He should be her enemy, considering he wanted to buy her father's house and she refused to sell it. She should probably despise him as much as she despised Moreen. But she didn't.

In fact, as she remembered him coming to her room last night and consoling her, she was dangerously close to liking him, a lot.

Camille groaned as memories of her falling apart in front of him rushed to the surface. He probably should have been disgusted by that display, but instead he'd stayed with her. What surprised her most about that little exchange was that he actually had been successful in calming her. Nobody had ever been able to calm her through an attack that way except her father. His gentle touch remained as her cheek tingled. Then with a start she sat up and looked down at herself. With a relieved sigh she noticed that she still wore her slacks and blouse from yesterday. So nothing had happened between her and Adam. At least nothing that she would be forever embarrassed about. The episode was small fries compared to what she'd been thinking in the last few minutes.

Now aware of her surroundings and the reason for her being there she did get up with the intention of going to the phone to find out how early the shops on the first floor opened. She hadn't planned on staying in Vegas so she hadn't brought so much as an overnight bag with her. She paused at the note placed on top of the phone.

Meeting's at noon. A car will be downstairs to pick you up. Patrice, in the gift shop downstairs has been instructed to take care of

whatever you need. She assured me that she
had a huge selection of CK Davis Designs in
stock.
Adam

Camille had to smile at that last sentence. She
really did want Adam Donovan to be her enemy. It
would make her decision not to sell her father's
house a lot easier. But Adam had been nothing but
nice to her, probably too nice.

Her cell phone chimed as Camille held the note
in her hand, contemplating her feelings. She still
held the slip of paper as she moved to her purse and
retrieved the phone.

"Camille Davis."

"Where are you? I've been calling your apartment all night. I wanted to find out how things went
with Moreen," Dana said in one breath. For years
Camille had wondered how a person could talk so
fast without being winded.

Moving to the couch Camille plopped down and
laid her head back. "I'm still in Vegas."

"What? Why? Did she kidnap you?"

Camille chuckled. "You are so dramatic. No,
she didn't kidnap me. I interrupted the meeting
before anything could be signed but then one of the
buyers asked me to dinner to discuss the deal
further."

"He asked you to dinner?"

Camille wondered why Dana assumed the

buyer was a man and could hear the shift in her friend's tone.

"Was he cute?" Dana asked with growing excitement.

Camille couldn't resist a smile. "Yes, he's cute. But that's not why I went to dinner with him."

"If he was cute then that should have been the only reason you went with him. You already know you don't want to sell the house. Why even entertain his offer?"

Camille was asking herself the same question. And the only answer she could come up with was that she wanted a chance to be with Adam Donovan again. "As it turns out I knew him."

"Really? Who is he?"

Camille groaned inwardly, knowing that the moment she released this tidbit of information Dana was going to flip her lid. "Remember the guy we saw in the casino, the one you wanted me to do?"

"Stop playing! Girl, that fine-ass man is the one trying to buy your property?" Dana practically squealed. "I'd sell him something all right."

"I just bet you would. If you weren't happily married, that is. Speaking of which, is Carl back from Phoenix?"

"Yeah, he got back last night. But I don't want to talk about that. I want to hear about the dinner you had with that hunk."

"The hunk's name is Adam Donovan," Camille

said, trying to hide a smile. Although she was only on the phone with Dana she was smiling so hard it was bound to be heard in her voice. "And he seems really nice. It's a shame I have to kill his deal. But he's not starving for money so I guess he'll be okay."

"Maybe you should prolong your decision, spend a few more days in Vegas getting to know Adam and…" Dana's voice trailed off.

Camille quickly picked up her drift. "Not happening. I'm meeting with him and his partner at noon. I guess Moreen will be there, too. At any rate, I'm going to put an end to this deal once and for all. I should be back in L.A. tonight."

"What you should do is cancel that meeting, have a little fun with Adam, then kill the deal and come home."

"That's cruel."

Dana chuckled. "That's life. Men do it all the time, Camille. Stop being so uptight. You know that guy was feeling you when we were at the bar that night and I'm sure he's more than happy to have run into you again. Get yourself a little somethin' somethin' and then go back to business. You deserve it."

"And what about him? Does he deserve a one-night stand?" Not that Camille was even considering this idea.

"Like I said, men do it all the time. I'm sure he's done it a few times, as well. And I'm not saying it has to be just a one-night stand. I know how you are about sex and commitment. I'm just saying you should explore your options with this guy and see where things might lead."

Camille sighed. "They might lead to him cursing me out since he paid for my hotel stay and is apparently footing the bill for my wardrobe for the day since I didn't plan on staying here. I'm sure he could say it was just business and write it off as that but it's going to be crappy that I'm not going through with his deal after all this."

"I've been meaning to ask you about that, Camille. Why won't you sell the house? You have no plans on living there. Is it just to get back at Moreen?"

"No!" Camille answered quickly. "I don't know," she sighed. "It just seems like it's too soon to let it go. To let him go."

"But he is gone, Camille. Keeping that house isn't going to bring him back."

"I know," she said sadly. Her stomach growled and Camille instantly thought of the meager dinner she'd had and the breakfast she craved. Scrambled eggs, bacon, pancakes and orange juice sounded divine. Then she let the hand with the note from Adam fall to her stomach and felt the cushiony softness. Yogurt and fruit would have to suffice.

"I'd better get ready for the meeting. I'll call you later with my flight info so you can pick me up," she told Dana.

"Okay, but remember what I said, Camille.

Take a chance for once, give yourself an early Christmas gift."

Camille disconnected with Dana with every intention of ignoring her friend's advice.

She'd tried on a dozen or so business suits and an equal amount of dresses and wasn't totally satisfied with any of them. While the boutique was very well stocked and carried a lot of her designs, Camille just couldn't seem to find the right outfit. Everything made her look fat. A`part of her knew it was just the complex she'd had all her life and that the size twelve outfits didn't look that bad on her, but then another part remembered that Moreen would be at that meeting.

Moreen would be dressed in something chic and expensive and she'd look gorgeous and skinny with her svelte size-six body. Today, of all days, Camille needed to be one hundred percent. She needed to feel like she owned the world along with half her father's house. Moreen would be angry and that would make her sharper, more vindictive and nastier than usual. Max Donovan would no doubt be on point after having spoken to his company lawyers and real estate appraisers again. And then there was Adam.

Adam would be handsome and debonair and charming. All the things he'd been last night and then some. Yeah, she definitely had to be ready for this meeting. And a glance at her watch told her if she didn't pick an outfit and hustle upstairs to her room she'd start off by being late, which wasn't a good thing.

An hour later and twenty minutes ahead of schedule Camille stepped out of the Gramercy to a seasonally warm October day. She'd settled on the charcoal gray silk suit with the knee-length flared skirt and fitted jacket that covered her too-round bottom. Sassy Milano pumps gave her height, which ultimately made her appear slimmer, while the excellent cut of the jacket concealed any bulging at her waist and accented her generous bosom. She felt professional, yet attractive and sure of her appearance for a change.

One of her company's mottos was to do just that. To provide clothes that appealed to every woman of all sizes and classes, to make each woman feel sexy and self-assured. The weird thing was that for the majority of her life, Camille hadn't felt any of those things herself. It had been only in the last five years that she'd begun to gain some sense of confidence. And while it wasn't much, she had learned to take her victories in small doses.

Besides, this meeting would be over quickly and then she'd be on her way back to L.A. She had a show to do in two weeks. This little trip was putting her behind schedule and that too was beginning to worry her. There were so many things that still needed to be done. Meetings with the technicians at the theater where the fashion show was being held, last minute alterations and changes to the lineup, model contracts and the reception for three hundred of L.A.'s high-class society and the press. She could not afford these two days away from her office, yet it was necessary.

They arrived at the building before Camille had her game plan in order. On the ride over, after she'd pushed aside CK Davis Designs business, she'd begun to think about why she was here in Vegas. Her father's house. The house where she'd grown up, where she'd had the best times with her father. Now her father was gone and if she didn't stop it, his house would be, too. How did she really feel about that? Extremely sad, she admitted. Tears stung her eyes and she tried to take deep breaths to hold them at bay.

She stepped onto the elevator and let her head fall back against the wall. "Don't cry. Don't cry," she chanted over and over until she thought she had herself under control.

The meeting was starting in ten minutes and she still hadn't arrived. Adam had tried not to appear nervous. He wasn't nervous. She was just a woman, just a client actually. And after today, after she signed over her share in the house, she wouldn't even be that. He could stand here and try to convince himself that this would be the end of their involvement but that would be stupid and a waste of time. And if there was one thing Adam Donovan did not believe in doing it was wasting time.

Last night she'd appealed to him on a level he hadn't even known existed in his mind. She'd needed him in a way he'd never been needed before. She was having some type of breakdown and he'd been there for her. He hadn't a clue what he was doing at the time, however. All he knew was that she was in trouble and he was determined to help her. Afterwards she'd seemed to open up a little more. She laughed and she talked—not too much about herself—but she'd seemed very interested in his childhood and his family life. They'd talked for a while until she just about collapsed from exhaustion. He'd watched her sleep for a few minutes there on the couch with her legs in his lap, her head cradled by her arm resting on the back of the chair.

She looked stressed even in her sleep. He'd brushed his hand over her forehead, trying to smooth away the worry lines there but had been unsuccessful. Whatever it was that bothered her so deeply attacked her even in sleep.

This morning he'd awakened with a tense body and a mind still full of Camille Davis. He wanted to call her, to offer to have breakfast with her. Anything, because he'd felt desperate to see her. But then Max had called wanting to meet with him alone before their meeting with the Davis women.

He'd been in this building for four hours already and was itching to see Camille, to at least talk to her. After finally finding a reasonable excuse to

leave Max's office Adam had headed for the eleva-
tors. He was pacing in front of the doors, his hands
in both pockets of his pants as he waited for the
elevator to arrive. His shoes clicked against the
marble floor and he wondered what was taking
Camille so long. It was his plan to ride downstairs,
to look for Virgil and his car and then to call the
hotel if need be.

He heard the ding signaling that the elevator was
there and stopped directly in front of it. The doors
opened and his heart gave a staggered beat.

Camille stood against the wall, her eyes closed
tightly, her hands gripping the handrail until her
knuckles turned white. Of course he rushed to her side
and of course he touched her, it would have taken an
army of men to prevent him from doing otherwise.

His hands covered hers as he tried to pull them
off the rails. "What is it?" he whispered.

Camille's eyes shot open and searched his face
for recognition. Adam felt the moment she realized
who he was. It was a flash of heat, pooled in the
center of her pupils. Then the heat melted away to
be replaced by surprise and then indignation. "I
am fine. Let me go," she said in a voice that was
way too shaky for his liking.

"You're shaking. Who upset you?" She smelled
delicious and looked fantastic. He'd noticed her
stylish beauty that first night and then yesterday
he'd watched her natural feminism blossom in front
of him. Today, she was sophisticated, alluring.

"I am fi—"

"Don't lie to me, Camille," he interrupted. He captured her gaze and held it, letting her know he was serious and that her claims of being okay were not fooling him. "Tell me what's wrong?" he said in a calmer tone even though his body shook with anger that he couldn't quite place.

"I was just thinking of something that made me sad. That's all. I am really fine now." She tried to move around him when the elevator doors closed. "Great," she said in an exasperated tone as she pushed the button to try and open them again.

It was too late; the elevator was already moving again. She sighed and rested her forehead on the doors.

Adam walked up behind her and placed his hands on her shoulders. "Were you thinking of your father?"

She didn't answer but he felt her shoulders tense.

"It's okay to be sad about losing him, Camille. If something happened to my father I'd be crushed. You can cry, it doesn't make you weak."

"Crying won't bring him back," she said softly.

"No," he said stroking her arms. "It won't. But sometimes a good cry is just what a body needs to rejuvenate itself and move on."

She inhaled and exhaled deeply. "I am not going to cry. I just want to get this meeting over with so I can go home."

Adam reached around her and pushed the

number to the floor the meeting was on. "Then we will make it quick."

They stood in the quiet for a second or so, then Adam took a deep breath himself, filling his body with her scent as he did. For a minute he was dizzy with wanting her. Then he shook his head to clear those thoughts. "What do you want to do about the house, Camille? Whatever you want, I'll respect."

Camille sighed. Her traitorous body had been on fire since the moment he'd stepped onto this elevator. She'd wanted to fall into his arms when she'd opened her eyes and saw him looking down at her. He was so close, his body offering a shield of protection she had always longed for. But then she remembered who he was and what he wanted and who she was and what she wanted. She did not need a protector and she did not want Adam Donovan feeling as if she were indebted to him in any way.

But then he'd said something that once again had changed her thoughts where he was concerned. She'd come here today with the express intention of ending this deal. She would keep her father's house and buy Moreen's share if need be. She would not sell to this man who had already admitted to fixing up properties and selling them for profit. She did not want her father's house in someone else's hands. But, as Dana and Moreen had reminded her, she had no intentions of living in it herself. While she wanted the memory to exist in her mind, she in no way thought she could handle facing it on a daily basis.

So where did that leave her? What did she want to do with the house?

He would respect her wishes. What kind of businessman said that? And did he mean it?

She turned slowly until she was facing him. He was still very close, so much so that his silky gray tie was at direct eye level with her. She reached out and touched it because she had always loved a good tie. Her father wore expensive ties of the most original colors. Adam did not move and she was careful to keep her fingers from actually grazing his chest. She looked up into his eyes then and saw something there she hadn't wanted to accept.

Adam Donovan had caring eyes to go along with this compassion that he'd shown her on two occasions now. He was dangerously handsome with his close cut curly black hair and cleft chin. His body was broad, like most of the male models she hired and yet he did not appear to be ruled by his good looks. That was a rarity in her world. In the world of fashion people who looked like Adam knew they were the bomb and commanded healthy paychecks because of it. Adam already had a boatload of money and he looked too good to be true. But that wasn't any of her business.

She pulled her hands away from him and asked. "What will you do with the house if I sell it to you? I mean, specifically, what will you do to it?"

"A complete renovation beginning with the main

hall and extending all the way out to the landscape. It's a great piece of land but it isn't being displayed to its best advantage. I have several designers that I work with exclusively but I'm thinking of one in particular who is a master with Asian décor."

Camille studied him. "The high ceilings," she said slowly. "That is what I like best about the house. When I was a little girl I used to pretend it was my castle."

He touched her chin then her cheek and she struggled not to lean into him. "The princess," he whispered.

He looked at her as if she were the only person in the world and she liked it. She wondered what he saw, if it were the fat girl who couldn't get enough of her father's attention or the business-woman who spent her time dressing other females because she was so ashamed of her own body. Those were her therapist's words. Questions she'd asked Camille. Questions Camille still could not answer.

"I was never a princess," she responded. "More along the lines of Cinderella, I would say."

"Cinderella was a princess, a beautiful one who was rescued by the dashing prince at the ball."

He still touched her face and this time Camille did lean her head into his touch. Just for a moment she'd allow herself the fantasy.

Then the elevator dinged and the doors opened

again. She pulled away from him then and stepped off. She heard him behind her and turned back to face him.

"I won't sell you the house."

Chapter 3

Adam tried not to react to her words. They bothered him, there was no denying that, but he doubted she needed to hear that. Instead he nodded in concession, then took her arm and led her towards the conference room.

"Where are we going?" she asked when he'd all but dragged her several steps.

"To the meeting. Once we're all gathered you can tell everyone what you've decided." And he could watch Max die a slow death when she did. This was a multimillion-dollar deal for Donovan Investments and a huge blow to their ego if it did not go through.

"But I want to tell you first." She slowed down as they approached the door.

Adam clenched his teeth to keep from speaking too harshly to her. He really couldn't understand why she was keeping the house if she had no intention of ever using it again. If it were just because she wanted a piece of her father then she was doing him a grave disservice, as well. That house and that property deserved to be more than a shrine. "You've already told me," he grumbled.

"No." She stopped, pulling her arm out of his grip. "I haven't told you all of it."

Adam took a deep breath and faced her. "You don't want to sell the house. I have no choice but to accept that." He hadn't wanted to look at her, hadn't wanted that connection with her again but found his gaze resting on those slanted eyes of hers and knew he was going to give in. "Tell me the rest, Camille."

She clasped her hands in front of her and fidgeted for a second, then seemed to pull herself together and looked at him seriously. "I want us to be partners. I mean, in this deal. I agree that the house has a lot of potential that it's not reaching and I'd like to see it renovated. My expertise is in dressing men and women, not houses. And since Donovan Investments apparently has a good track record in renovating properties I think we could work well together."

Adam shook his head. "I don't understand. I buy

houses, fix them up and sell them. And you're suggesting some sort of partnership in just renovation. That's not what we do."

Her hair was cut in a neat bob scraping the line of her jaw. When a strand slipped dangerously close to her mouth she lifted her hand and tucked it back behind her ear. The right side of her face was left bare; her high cheekbone and lightly shaded eye were completely exposed. But he was not going to be distracted by her exotic good looks.

"I'll pay for half the renovations and as an investment you can pay for the other half. Once the work is done we'll have the house appraised again and I'll decide if I'm going to sell it to you."

"And what happens when you decide you still want to keep the house for yourself?"

"I'll pay you your investment back."

Adam was stunned. At this time yesterday he'd been headed into a meeting that he thought was an open-and-shut deal. Now there were too many elements for him to keep track of. There was the beautiful, yet complicated woman, the stepmother who he wasn't so sure was on the up-and-up and now this. "Why would I be interested in an investment, Camille? I can just as easily find another property and go about my business the usual way. There's really no reason why I should give this deal of yours a second thought."

"You met my father. You saw what that house meant to him and I've told you what it means to me.

Are you just a ruthless businessman with his eye only on the money to be made? Or do you have some real passion for what you do?"

It was issued as a challenge. That alone had knocked Adam further off kilter. A few minutes ago she was trembling in his arms, now she was standing toe to toe with him as if they were in a fight for their lives. "I admit that the house has a lot of potential, so much so that I couldn't wait to get my hands on it. But I want it for myself."

An elegant brow arched as she glared at him and heat raced to Adam's groin. "Selfish, are we?"

He shrugged. "More like greedy." He took a step closer to her. "You see, Camille, when I see something I want I stop at nothing to obtain it. And once I have it, it's mine until I'm ready to let it go."

To her credit she did not flinch and Adam grew even more aroused. "That's a habit I'm sure you can stand to break, Adam. I'm offering you a partnership. I know how much that house is worth and I'm sure that with renovations that price would be tripled. You strike me as a gambling man so there's no way you're going to let this opportunity slip through your fingers because of a technicality."

"The fact that you will still own the house I pour my heart into renovating is not a technicality. There's no guarantee that at the end of the project I'll see that triple profit."

"And there's no guarantee that you won't."

Before he could refute that statement the door to the conference room opened and Max joined them.

"I was wondering if I was going to have to send a search party for you two. Can we get this meeting going? I'm sure Ms. Davis has her own business to tend to back in L.A.," he said in a clipped tone.

Adam watched as Camille smiled at Max. "You're absolutely right, Mr. Donovan. I'm ready to begin."

She slipped past him and Adam felt his whole body tremble. Never before had he been affected by a woman like this. She confused him, she intrigued him, she baffled and impressed him. Rubbing a hand down his face he tried to fight off the feeling that he was sinking in quicksand.

"You okay?" Max asked, clapping him on the back.

Adam turned but avoided Max's assessing gaze. "I'm fine. Let's get this over with."

Camille entered the conference room knowing that Adam was right behind her and knowing that she'd confused the hell out of him. She'd even confused herself. She had come to this meeting with the express intention of telling them she would not sell and now she was thinking differently. While she wasn't quite sure she wanted to sell the property outright she knew that she would love nothing more than to see it renovated.

Moreen had been too busy spending her father's

money on herself to make sure the house was in the shape it should be. Camille always felt that if her mother had lived their home would have been grand and warm with love. Instead it was just big, full of rooms and expensive things but no real feeling, except for the memories she kept locked in her mind.

When she took a seat Camille noticed Moreen looking at her with her normal disdain. Camille put her purse on the table and sat up as straight as possible in the low-backed chair. Today was not the day to be cowed. Instead she turned to her stepmother and managed a cool smile. "Good afternoon."

Moreen frowned. "That color does nothing for you. It makes your skin look dull and drab."

Camille kept her smile in place and watched as Adam and Max took their seats across the table.

Moreen moved in closer and whispered viciously, "And that jacket is too small. You'd think you would know what size you wear by now."

"Can I get you some coffee or something?" Max asked Camille since he'd already gotten Mrs. Davis a drink while they waited.

Camille tried to ignore Moreen's comment but felt her hands shaking as she moved her purse from in front of her off to the side of where she sat. "Yes, please. I'd like some water."

"I'll get it," Adam said before Max had a chance to move. He stood and Camille watched his well-built body in that expertly cut suit and remembered how it felt when he'd held her last night.

Take a chance for once, she remembered Dana saying.

It makes your skin look dull and drab, Moreen's words echoed over Dana's.

Adam put the glass in front of her and touched her shoulder. She jumped slightly then looked up at him. "Thanks," she whispered.

"Take a sip then we'll get started," he told her.

His gaze held hers as she brought the glass up to her lips and swallowed slowly. Camille wasn't sure if it was the cool liquid sliding down her dry throat or the steady hand of the man standing behind her on her shoulder. In any case her heart rate slowed to a normal rhythm and she looked over at Max.

"Your partner and I were just discussing a slight modification to your proposal," she said in a confident voice.

Max lifted a brow and looked towards Adam who was moving back to his seat. "Modification?"

"Yes, it appears that Ms. Davis has some ideas of her own where her father's house is concerned. I think we should hear her out."

Adam gave her a nod and she warmed all over. He hadn't really said if he agreed with the idea but at least he wasn't shutting her down totally. He was giving her the floor to speak and she prayed she could handle it.

Of course she could handle it. She was Camille Davis of CK Davis Designs. She designed thousand-dollar dresses for Hollywood's elite, she made a seven-figure salary, had been featured in several magazines and supervised over sixty models per show. Surely she could handle herself in this room with three people, even if one of them was Moreen.

"Adam touched on something last night while we were at dinner that had me thinking. My father's house is a great property with lots of potential to make a bundle of money. Outside of that it has good structure and the potential to be a beautiful home. That said, I would like to be a part of making that a reality," she said and watched as Adam sat back in his chair, his warm eyes settling on her.

"What are you talking about? Are we selling the house to them or not?" Moreen protested.

Max hadn't spoken yet. Camille recognized mild interest in what she was saying so she continued. "The property won't be sold to Donovan Investments, yet. I'm offering to foot the bill for half the renovations and Donovan Investments can put up the other half. At the end of the project I'll decide if I want to sell the property."

"You'll decide. Just wait a minute here, missy. You don't call all the shots. Half of that house is mine and I say we sell now. I don't want to be burdened with that property any longer," Moreen huffed.

Camille turned to her quickly. "Then you can sell me your share and I'll do with it what I want."

Before an argument could break out Max held up a hand and said, "Wait a minute, I have a couple of questions. Ms. Davis, you have more than enough money to renovate that house yourself. Why even offer us the opportunity to invest if you don't want to sell to us?"

"Call me Camille," she said with a quick smile. "You're willing to pay whatever amount we ask for the property. Therefore I have to assume that you believe this is a good investment for your company. I know I have the money to do this myself but I don't have the time or the expertise that you and Adam do. You would have full control over the contractors and the renovation project with some minor input on my part. This way both of our visions for this property can hopefully come to fruition."

"But in the end if you don't decide to sell it to us," Max said, "then what?"

She looked at Adam thinking he would jump in at any moment. But he didn't. He just watched her in that cool, amused way of his. She did not falter. "If I decide to keep the house after the renovation I will pay your investment back, with interest. So it's not like you're going to lose money. Actually, it puts you in a win, win situation. Either way you'll make some sort of profit."

Max was rubbing his chin. "But it won't be as big a profit as if you just sold us the house outright."

Finally feeling relaxed and like this idea could

quite possibly go through, Camille sat back in her chair. "To the contrary, I'm saving you the initial output of money. You won't have to pay the two point five million I would ask for the house in addition to all the renovation costs. This way you'll put up five hundred thousand at the most right off the bat with the potential of either getting a twenty percent increase on your return or—"

"Or giving you four million dollars, which the house will undoubtedly be appraised for when the renovations are done," Adam finished.

So now he decided to speak; well, she still wasn't backing down. "Thereafter, you would ultimately sell the house for seven point five million, still making yourself a huge profit. So you see, you win either way."

"This is ridiculous!" Moreen stood. "You have no idea what you're doing. These men are professionals in real estate. We should sell for the two point five and get the hell out of here. Who wants to be bothered with renovations anyway?"

"I do," Camille said quietly.

Adam was watching her but Max was looking down at the folder in front of him. She wondered what he was thinking but found herself more enraptured by the intense gaze between her and Adam.

What was it about this man that made her warm all over? Not just warm, excited, empowered. He could have shot her deal down before they even entered this meeting and then again when they sat down but he'd given her the floor. He'd trusted that she could present this deal without making a fool of herself. Camille didn't receive that type of trust often and she appreciated it. She intended to let Adam know as soon as the meeting was over.

"I think it's a gamble. She strikes me as being too emotional and too personally attached to this house to let it go," Max was telling Adam when they'd stepped outside to talk it over. "But I can't deny that she's smart. I checked into the history of her company last night and she's built herself a small fortune without the help of her father. That tells me she knows how to do business."

Adam nodded. "I agree."

Max looked at him questioningly. "Is that all you have to say, that you agree?"

No, that wasn't all he had to say but what was going through his mind was only meant to be heard by one person and she looked a lot better than his brooding cousin. "She told me about the idea on the elevator. I was a little shocked at first but after hearing her talk I think it's a good one. In reality we can't make them sell that house to us. But if we invest in the renovation there's still the possibility that in that time she'll get over her mourning and let ûs have it."

"So you think this is all about her mourning the loss of her father?" Max asked.

Adam slipped his hands into his pockets. "I'm pretty sure it is." Along with other things, he thought, things that Max didn't need to know. Adam sensed that Camille needed to take this stand, not only against them for trying to buy the house without her permission but against her step-mother. There was no love lost between the two of them, of that he was sure. "Besides, I've wanted to get my hands on that house for too long to let it slip away now. Even if I only get the chance to renovate it I'll be satisfied."

"But what if she sells it on her own at the end of all this? She'll get the profit and we'll get a measly hundred grand."

"It's not about the money, Max."

Max frowned. "It's not? Since when? That's our business, Adam. We buy properties, fix them up and then sell them for a lot of money. That's the bottom line."

"Not this time," Adam said solemnly.

This time it was about something else, or should he say someone else. It was about this woman and the thoughts she'd put into his mind since the first moment he'd seen her. Adam wanted her in his bed, but that was the easy part. He also wanted her trust, her confidence. He had no clue why but wasn't in the habit of second guessing himself either.

"Let's do this deal and see where it takes us," he said to Max. "Like she said, we win either way."

"Yeah," Max said slowly, keeping a close eye on his younger cousin, "but which one of us is going to win bigger?"

Moreen tossed her head back and laughed. Camille recognized the sound and stood, crossing the room to stand near the window.

"Just what do you really think you're doing?" Moreen asked.

Camille kept her back to her, drawing strength in the fact that she didn't have to face her. "I thought I was speaking in plain English so I'm not sure what you aren't understanding."

"This isn't about that house. Oh, no, I think it's about much more than that."

"I don't know what you're talking about, Moreen. If you don't want to go along with it then I'll buy your half of the house and you can be on your way." *Then my life would be so much simpler.*

"I'll speak in plain English for you. He's rich, he's handsome, he's got playboy written all over him. Besides the fact that you could never handle that type of man, Adam Donovan would not be caught dead with a woman like you."

With those words Camille spun around and glared at Moreen. She was, as expected, dressed in a sophisticated burnt-orange suit with her purse, hat and shoes matching. She wore jewelry, not gaudy, but tasteful diamonds at her ears, neck and on her

fingers. She was cool and chic and sexy and
Camille was slightly intimidated.

But she was also angry. "First of all, I couldn't
care less what type of man Adam Donovan is. This
is a business deal and if it weren't for you I
wouldn't even be here trying to pull this off." She
took a step closer to Moreen because she wanted
to prove to the mean woman and herself that she
wasn't afraid to. "And furthermore, what do you
mean a woman like *me?* There is nothing wrong
with me."

She said the words, felt the power of them
washing over her and wanted to scream with
victory. But then Moreen laughed again, effectively
cutting down Camille's triumph.

"You are small potatoes compared to the
polished allure he's used to. You're frumpy, disguis-
ing it only in the expensive clothes you design. You
dress the most beautiful women in the world but
you aren't one of them."

Camille's heart raced and her fists clenched at
her sides. She could hit Moreen. She could get one
good swing off and watch her skinny, toned body
fall to the floor. But what good would that do?
Moreen would only laugh at her again.

"Is everything all right in here?"

Adam's voice echoed in her head and Camille
took a shaky step back. She found his eyes and
knew instinctively that he would know something
was wrong with her and would undoubtedly try to

come to her rescue, again. He was beginning to be very good at that.

"I'm fine," she was saying but he'd already started walking towards her. She took a step back so that he wouldn't touch her. The last thing she wanted to do was put on a show for Moreen. The old witch would get way too much pleasure out of watching Camille melt from Adam's touch.

He must have sensed her further discomfort because he didn't reach for her like she knew he wanted to. Instead he turned to Moreen and said curtly, "Have a seat so we can finish this."

Moreen acted as if she were adjusting her clothes before regally lowering herself into the chair.

Camille took a deep breath and was about to cross the room to where she had been sitting previously when Adam took her by the elbow and guided her to the chair at the other end of the table. Once she was seated he sat beside her and waited while Max closed the door.

"We will invest in the renovations of the house with you," Adam said seriously, looking from Camille to Moreen.

"On two conditions," Max added.

"This is insane." Moreen swore.

Camille and everyone else in the room ignored her. "What are the conditions?" Camille asked.

"We, Donovan Investments, will have the final

say on all renovations. We will gladly consult you on initial ideas but the final say will be ours."

Adam quickly jumped in. "You said yourself that you do not have the expertise in this area. We do. If we are going to invest in this project we have to know that it will be done right."

Camille looked at both men. There was a resemblance there. Along the lines of their jaw, the broad shoulders, the self-assured stance and almost arrogant air they both emitted. They were both extremely handsome, Max with those dreamy eyes and Adam with his easygoing charm. But there was no doubt which one she was drawn to.

Camille sighed with that admission. She'd tried to fight it, tried to ignore it, but it was no use. She was more than attracted to Adam Donovan. And that, she knew, was a big mistake.

"I trust your judgment," she said finally when her thoughts threatened to break her out into a sweat.

"The second condition is that Donovan Investments be given the first option to buy the property in the event that you decide to sell."

Camille looked at Max then because it was easier to keep her cool. "Absolutely."

Max smiled. "Then I guess we have a deal."

Camille smiled in return. "I guess we do."

Adam reached out and clasped her hand. "Congratulations. You're an excellent negotiator."

His eyes were saying something else and Camille was listening, however foolish.

"Is anybody going to ask me what I think of this deal?" Moreen asked in a huff.

"Pardon us, Mrs. Davis. We just assumed that you were in agreement," Max said. "But if you have something further you wish to discuss, we can do so."

Moreen waved a hand. "Just advise me when I can expect a check."

Camille turned to her instantly. "I've offered to buy your share."

Moreen stood and glared down at her. "And I am declining *your* offer."

Adam released Camille's hand and stood. "Then I guess you will be waiting until the renovations are completed for your payday just like us, Mrs. Davis. Our attorneys will keep you posted," he said by way of dismissal.

Camille just knew that Moreen was going to have a hot retort for him but was surprised when the old crow smiled in what she thought was a sweet way and extended her hand to Adam. "I am sure you will do your job expertly, Mr. Donovan. I only wish we could have wrapped this up without all the fanfare."

Adam shook her hand. "Actually I think this will be a very enjoyable partnership."

"If you say so," Moreen crooned before turning toward Max who had come around to her side of the table.

"I'll walk you out, Mrs. Davis," he said politely.

"Thank you, Mr. Donovan. You are both such handsome gentlemen. I'm sure your mothers are very proud."

"Yes, they are," Max said then tossed Adam a baleful look over his shoulder.

Adam grinned and nodded as they left the room.

Immediately Camille let her head fall into her hands. "She's going to drive me straight into the nut house."

Adam came to stand behind her, putting both hands on her shoulders and leaning over to speak into her ear. "Not if you don't let her."

Camille shook her head. "She just gets to me, that's all. She's done it for years."

"You've let her do it for years," Adam said then helped her to stand. "Stop giving her the ammunition to hurt you."

His hands went around her waist as if they belonged there and she, to her own horror, moved closer to him bringing her hands to rest on his shoulders. The position felt right, it felt comforting. "Old habits die hard," she said with a frown.

"Then I think it's time I help you develop some new habits."

Camille didn't have a moment to protest before his lips came down on hers. He covered her mouth with smooth finesse. A practiced move she was sure, but one that undoubtedly had the woman of choice swooning. At least it did with her.

As if it were the most natural thing in the world

her lips parted for his and when his tongue slipped inside her mouth hers wrapped around it in a twirl of sensual heat. He pulled her close as he deepened the kiss. Camille tilted her head and opened her mouth wider to receive this sweet torture.

On and on it seemed to go, his tongue stroking hers. Her moans echoing throughout the room. He nibbled her bottom lip and she shivered. His tongue glided over her teeth and her fingers flexed in the material of his suit jacket.

She was dizzy and way too hot to be wearing all the clothes she was wearing. Her heart beat rapidly but she didn't feel the urge to be sick or to run for cover. Instead she felt a sort of freedom that threatened to overtake her, threatened to have her stripping for him right here in this office.

He pulled away breathing as heavily as she was and rested his forehead against hers.

"This could easily turn from a habit to an addiction," she whispered.

His hands moved past her waist to cup her bottom. "I'm counting on it."

Chapter 4

"I'm booked on the five o'clock flight," Camille said when she was once again in the limo, this time with Adam sitting next to her.

"Then we have more than enough time to get something to eat," Adam replied.

He should have been in the office meeting with Max about work permits and what they would do first with the house. He needed to call the architect and send the designer on a buying trip as soon as possible. And he was positive that his brothers would want to hear about the results of the meeting, although he was sure Max had already called to fill them in.

There were pros and cons to belonging to a big family. He only had two brothers but his mother had two sisters and a brother, and his father had two brothers, which meant they had children and all the cousins were pretty close. So there was virtually nothing that went on in the life of one Donovan that all the Donovans didn't find out within a day or so.

Generally Adam didn't let that stress him. At the lowest point in his life all that family closeness had been his saving grace. Linc, being the older Donovan brother, had arrived in his room that first night after the demise of Adam's relationship with Kim Alvarez. He'd told him to be a man, to take those conflicting emotions and channel them into something that would pay off in the end, business. Linc was totally focused on business and becoming successful, at least he had been until he'd met his wife. Adam smiled at the memory of the spirited Jade Vincent, the woman who'd tamed his dominating playboy brother.

Trent had been a little more blunt in telling Adam to suck it up and find the next available pair of legs to climb between. But then that was Trent's way. He was an ex-navy Seal, a tactical man with basic divide-and-conquer ideas. There wasn't a woman on this earth that could do battle with Trent and Adam pitied each woman who had ever tried.

Max was his cousin but had been as close to Adam as a brother. The first of the Donovans to take Adam and his business ideas seriously and older than Adam by two years, Max had a strong influence on him. Adam wondered if allowing Camille's changes into this business deal may have disrupted his relationship with Max, but then thought better of it. Donovans were loyal to a fault and they didn't let anyone or anything come between them. Max agreed with the deal, which meant he saw potential in it just like Adam did.

The problem was, Adam was beginning to see something else in his dealings with Camille Davis.

He liked her. A lot.

That could be both a bad and a good thing. That analysis, however, would have to wait. Camille wouldn't be in Vegas much longer, but while she was he intended to be with her every minute.

"I'm not hungry," Camille said quickly.

He lifted her hand in his and stroked his thumb over her smooth skin. She looked a little nervous so he touched her, enjoying the feel of her soft skin against his own. "What did you have for breakfast?" he asked in a slow, soothing voice.

She looked as if she were deeply contemplating her answer. It was a simple question and the mere fact that she had to concentrate so hard to answer it spoke volumes to him. "You did eat something before you came to the meeting, didn't you? I called room service for you myself before I left the hotel."

"Is that why they sent that buffet to my room?" She turned to him. "That was way too much food. I had a glass of juice and some fruit," she stated pointedly.

He nodded even though he wasn't pleased with her answer. "Then you *are* hungry. It's past lunchtime and I'm starving."

"Adam," she began.

He squeezed her hand gently. "Don't argue, Camille. You wouldn't want me to starve, would you?"

She gave him a smirk, then smiled. "You really are used to getting what you want, aren't you?"

He smiled in return. "It's a habit."

"I thought we were working on breaking habits."

When the car came to a stop Camille prepared to get out but was stopped by Adam's hand on her leg. "Virgil's just picking up our lunch," he told her.

Convincing herself that his hand on her leg wasn't causing her pulse to trip she blinked and asked, "We aren't going to a restaurant?"

"No. There's something I want you to see before you leave. It's sort of a long ride so we'll have lunch when we get there."

She quickly scooted across the seat, away from Adam. "I don't want to see your house, Adam."

If her words disturbed him Adam didn't let it show. Instead he straightened his tie and glanced out the window before giving her a serious look. "I wouldn't take you to my house without your permission, Camille. And there's no reason for you to be afraid of being alone with me."

"I'm not afraid," she said, although her heart was beating wildly in her chest. She wasn't afraid of him, per se. Mostly she was afraid of the rejection that would inevitably come. Moreen was right about one thing. Adam was a great-looking guy used to a certain type of woman. She'd never fit into his world or his life. There was no sense in her thinking otherwise. "I just wanted to make that clear."

"Make what clear? That you'd rather jump out of a car than go to my house?"

The look he gave her was casual but she could tell that he was bothered by her response. She couldn't allow herself to be concerned with that. Dealing with Adam Donovan was going to take all her strength. He obviously had more experience with man/woman relations than she did and she doubted that he'd ever been on the receiving end of rejection.

"We are together because of our business deal. I don't want there to be any illusions, on either of our parts."

He didn't move from his spot but crooked a finger, bidding her to slide next to him again. She did so very slowly because the attraction between them was too alluring to do otherwise. When she was still about a foot away he reached around her waist and pulled until she slid effortlessly into his side, their legs and arms touching. He lifted his hands and pushed her hair back so that he had a full, unfettered view of her face. "I deal in reality only. I know that we're together because of a business deal. But I also know that I'd like there to be more."

Camille let out a choked laugh and tried to hide her continued nervousness. "Spoiled and candid. I'm learning so much about you today, Mr. Donovan."

He smiled then lowered his mouth to hers. "Relax, Camille. I won't hurt you."

She shook her head. "Don't say that," she said seriously. "You have no way of knowing what you will and will not do in the future. I'd rather you not make promises that you don't know if you can keep."

Her trust would be hard to win, Adam realized. Everything he managed to get from her would take a lot of work. He never worked to get a woman.

Never.

And since he had no intention of keeping a woman he'd never given the option any thought. This situation was changing with each second he remained near her. She was different, he already knew that. She was intriguing and, if he allowed her, she could be a repeat down memory lane. Adam let his hands fall from her face and watched as she sat back against the seat.

An hour later they pulled onto a gravelly road. Through the window Adam saw the familiar sight of a skeleton house. Foundation and beams, work trucks and construction paraphernalia stretched over the hundreds of acres of land. The car came to a stop and Virgil pulled the back door open.

Adam stepped out first, then reached for Camille's hand. Her heels hit the gravel and she stumbled a bit as she stood. He held her hand tightly and then slipped an arm around her waist. "I forgot that the driveway hasn't been paved yet. It's not really conducive to high heels."

She looked up at him and frowned. "I'd say this place isn't conducive to a lunch date, either."

They'd taken a few steps, Virgil following behind them with their lunch. "Are we on a date?"

"No," Camille answered hastily. "This is a business meeting, I guess."

Adam smiled. She was terribly attractive, regardless of how much work she entailed. "Take your time, the road clears a bit just up here."

"What is this place?" Camille asked when it appeared they'd entered the front door of the structure.

"We'll eat on the back porch, Virgil. You can go on ahead while I show Ms. Davis around," Adam said.

When they were alone he turned to Camille. "This is a house that's being built by Donavan Investments. I wanted you to see it because I want you to understand that it's not all about money for me. Shall we?" he asked with a flourish of his hand.

Camille followed his lead, listening as he described what each room would be. Initially she'd thought it impossible to envision a house being in this spot that was presently only wood and nails.

But as Adam went into detail about each room, the décor, the feel, the meaning she began to visualize and looked forward to seeing the finished product.

"This will be the master bedroom," he said when they'd come to the last room on the second level. "Over here will be nothing but windows so the Vegas skyline can be seen clearly. Deep browns and beiges will be the color scheme, something comforting, soothing to create a refuge after a long day's work. I found some terrific wallpaper while I was in Italy last summer. It's cream with the barest hint of gold woven intricately throughout. It'll be fantastic in here."

Camille had been wandering around the open space as he talked. She saw the vision clearly, almost too clearly. "The bed will be here. Something big and inviting," she said while standing in the middle of the floor. Turning in a small circle she continued, "Maybe a mahogany wood or cedar to play off the brown color scheme. A fireplace should be in that corner with a sitting area for nightcaps before falling asleep."

She stopped when she caught Adam staring at her. "It's just a suggestion," she said shyly. "I really don't know much about decorating."

"But you know about color, about movement and feeling. What else do you see in here?" he prodded.

She shrugged and took a step toward another opening. "This should be the master bath. Marble tiles, maybe a champagne-and-gold color to go with the wallpaper in the other room. A deep jetted tub could be here. His and her sinks and plenty of counter space."

"His and her sinks?" Adam questioned.

"Women like their own space, especially in the bathroom." She smiled because he looked like he was enjoying what she was saying.

"There's something to be said about sharing space. The intimacy, the connection of two people forced to remain close to each other."

His voice had lowered until a deep whisper and she felt mesmerized by his words. "I've often wondered how close two people could actually become. If that shared-soul thing was just a myth. What do you think?"

This entire scene had been more than romantic, the empty room, the shared visions, the quietness of the desert around them. He'd been in a seductive mood watching her body as she moved throughout this space. One minute he wanted to rip her clothes off and make love to her on these bare floors and the next he was entranced in her words, wondering how she could so plainly see what was only in his mind.

He'd brought up intimacy and connection when he knew that he was incapable of both. A part of him presumed she'd shy away from the conversation the way she had shied away any time he mentioned something other than business. This time she'd shocked him. Tossing the ball firmly in his court. And he'd dropped it.

Thrusting his hands into his pockets he looked away and shrugged. "I guess it exists for people who are open to that type of involvement." That sounded good, didn't it? "I mean, if you're the type to look for soul partners and connections of that sort."

"What type are you?" she asked immediately.

"Excuse me?" he asked to buy himself some more time. It was suddenly really small in here.

"Are you into connections and soul partners or are you simply into the moment? I've known people that are both ways. I'd have to say that I respect people that are into the moment more."

He would have guessed her for the romantic soul-partner type, but then she was constantly surprising him. "Why?"

"I respect honesty. I don't like setting the scene to get what you want, then walking away as if you'd never been there. Get my drift?"

Boy, did he, and again he was amazed. Camille Davis could be shy and emotional. On the other hand she could be ambitious and very intuitive. "I'll keep that tidbit of information for later use," he said because he was sure that any other response would have been the wrong one.

Adam led her back downstairs to the back of the house where Virgil had set up a folding table with two chairs. The table was covered with a white linen cloth with a vase filled with peach roses in its center. Three crystal bowls held salads; chicken, turkey and macaroni, and a silver tray held a tower of sandwiches. In front of each chair was a china plate and a glass. A pitcher of fresh-squeezed lemonade and another of water rounded out the meal. With a nod of approval Adam dismissed Virgil.

"Did you fix a plate?" he asked the driver before he had a chance to leave them alone.

Virgil nodded positively and Adam smiled.

"You feed your employees. So you're not a heartless employer," Camille commented while taking a seat. Then her voice shifted with concern. "You didn't order any tossed salad."

"Sorry, you know I have bad memories about rabbit food." Adam took his seat and picked up her plate. "I'm glad you don't consider me heartless," he said as he scooped a spoonful of chicken salad onto her plate. He followed it with a scoop of each of the other salads, then picked up a half sandwich and set it on the plate. He watched her frown when he put the plate down in front of her. It both annoyed and concerned him.

"A salad would have been fine," she said.

Adam held her glare. "You only had fruit and juice for breakfast. That was about—" he looked at his watch "—five hours ago. I've given you three salads and a sandwich. You need to eat."

Camille pushed the plate away. "You're also bossy."

Adam chuckled. "You're developing quite a list

of my traits." He pushed the plate closer to her. "Eat, Camille." Adam picked up his plate and began to fill it with food.

"I'm not a child," she argued and pouted.

"Then stop acting like one."

She looked as if she wanted to say something else, to argue just a bit more. Then he presumed she thought better of it and with a frown picked up her fork and took a bite. A small measure of triumph spread through him and he happily continued to stack his own plate.

Camille sat on the plane staring out the window in deep thought. This trip had not gone the way she'd planned and yet it had been quite enjoyable.

She liked Adam. That was undeniable.

She liked the deal she'd struck with Donovan Investments even more. After touring the unfinished house with Adam and listening to his ideas she'd begun thinking of her father's house and all the wonderful things they could do to transform that space. She couldn't wait until the renovation began but now was trying to figure out how she was going to work that project in with her already busy schedule.

That brought her back to her own reality and she took out her organizer and PalmPilot, then called her office for messages. Dana was her partner at CK Davis Designs but Dana did mostly administrative stuff. Camille was the designer and so the clothes, models and fashion show were all hers. And she loved it. From the time she was thirteen and she'd returned from a shopping spree with Moreen angry and discouraged by the lack of pretty clothes designed for girls who weren't a perfect size zero to seven, she'd known that this was her calling.

By the time she was fourteen she'd already designed a complete winter collection for the slightly overweight teenage girl. And although she never shared her pictures with anyone it gave Camille great satisfaction to know that there was something she was good at. It wasn't until she was a junior in high school and Dana came across her box full of designs that the idea for CK Davis Designs was formed. Dana had an excellent head for business and the ambition and drive that Camille had yet to possess.

College quickly turned into design school where Camille perfected her already keen skills. She enrolled in a few business classes with Dana and began to feel her own sense of ambition rise. The thought of running her own business, of catering to all sizes—the forgotten ones—in a fashionable way in an effort to help boost their self-esteem became her sole focus. Her father's encouragement only solidified her career choice.

Today, CK Davis Designs was her heart and soul. It provided the type of therapy that money could never buy. She was doing something important, something that helped people like her. This fall she would release her first children's line and she was more than excited. It would be a success, she was sure of it. Too bad she wasn't that certain in other areas of her life.

Sofari, her assistant, had handled most of the routine calls but there were two emergencies she needed to deal with immediately upon her return. She was short on a fabric that was imperative to the evening gown collection and her male model order was in jeopardy due to two more fashion shows taking place the same week. She placed another call to her factory manager informing him that she'd be there first thing in the morning and to have all the samples ready for inspection and one final call to Dana to let her know what time she'd be landing.

Now she had about forty-five minutes to think about how she was going to get over this growing crush she had on Adam Donovan.

It was basically ridiculous that a twenty-nine-year-old woman could develop a crush on a man in one day. Actually, she could admit, to herself only, that this crush had developed months ago when she'd first bumped into Adam at the Gramercy Casino. Dreaming of him had been her secret, one she presumed she'd have for the rest of her natural life. She never imagined that she'd see him again, let alone be forced to work with him in any way.

She thought of the deal she'd struck and the possibility that she'd done it just to keep contact with him for a little while longer. She smiled to herself;

if only she were so brave to think of something like that. The deal was a result of her reluctance to let go of her father, the only person who ever loved her unconditionally. She just prayed that once the renovations were done she would be able to finally put that part of her life behind her.

Adam tapped into another one of her deficiencies. Relationships were not her specialty. In fact, they only seemed to remind her of all her shortcomings, so she didn't spend a lot of time on them. For once, she admitted, Moreen had been right, Adam wasn't in her league. Not just because he was rich, because she had money of her own. But Adam appeared to be the type of man used to having women, a certain type of women. Tall, skinny and beautiful immediately came to her mind. Three things Camille was not.

With a hand she smoothed down her jacket letting her palms rest on her thighs. She pulled her legs closer together so the spread wouldn't look as wide. It didn't work because she could only keep them that way for a few minutes. Briefly she entertained the thought that Adam didn't mind her extra curves. The lunch date and the trip to the house weren't strictly business. Camille was smart enough to know that. And Adam was clear on his intentions, well, mostly at least. He was attracted to her. The kiss in his office and again when he dropped her off at the airport proved that. Maybe he just wanted to sleep with her. Men who preferred tall, skinny women on their arms weren't really that particular about what type of woman was in their bed.

Unfortunately, Camille wasn't that type of woman. With all her self-esteem issues she'd held strong to one fact. If she were in a relationship with a man he would give her the respect she deserved. With that in mind she decided that it was imperative, where Adam Donovan was concerned, to preserve her dignity and to guard whatever unsolicited emotions she was developing for him carefully.

There were things in life that Camille needed, things she didn't expect any man to ever provide. She accepted that fact and the lonely fate it dictated for her. Yet she still had a life. She had a flourishing business and a friend who was as close as family. Those things would sustain her. They had to.

Adam returned to the office after dropping Camille off at the airport. On the ride over he'd thought about their afternoon together. To say he was intrigued by this woman was a grave understatement.

Women were one of his favorite pastimes. He liked them tall, short, employed, unemployed, pretty and not so pretty. He just liked women. Did that make him a bad guy? He didn't think so. So why did he feel like Camille was going to hold that against him?

He shouldn't be worried about how she thought

of him. Hell, she had most of his unfavorable traits down to a T. He smiled as he remembered her comment about him being bossy. He'd often accused his brothers of the same thing so he never figured himself for it.

Closing his eyes he allowed himself one more visual of her innocently pretty face and her deceptively sexy body. There were many contrasts where Camille Davis was concerned, the biggest, most blatant one being the complete naivety she exuded mentally while her voluptuous body spoke of great passion and experience physically. His groin tightened with the thought. Having experienced many women Adam had developed a special taste for soft feminine curves. Curves which Camille possessed an abundance of. He sensed that she wasn't all that comfortable with her body and couldn't help wanting to teach her all the ways to use that commodity to her advantage. He'd held her close, feeling her full, round breasts against him. He'd watched the sway of her hips until his eyes had almost been hypnotized and he'd imagined himself planted firmly between her thick thighs to the point of almost embarrassing her and himself with his overzealousness.

Yes, Camille Davis and that luscious body of hers would drive him insane. If he let her. Which he had no intention of doing.

There was a new deal on the table. One that

meant a lot to him, for reasons he wasn't quite ready to disclose.

"I see you've returned. What happened, you finally remembered there was business you needed to take care of?" Max said, coming into Adam's office and taking an unoffered seat.

Adam leaned back in his chair and sent a smirk Max's way. "Ha ha. Yes, I'm back. I just took her to the airport."

Max looked at his watch. "And how far away is the airport again?"

"The house. That's what you and I should be discussing, the Davis house," Adam said in no uncertain terms. Whatever was going on between him and Camille, which was nothing because he wasn't looking for a romantic entanglement with a person who he was doing business with, he wasn't about to discuss it with Max.

Max nodded knowingly. "Good, because that's exactly what I came in here to talk about. We can have an inspector in L.A. by the end of the week. Preliminarily I think the house is structurally sound. But the renovations I've got in mind are going to call for some demolition so I just want to make sure we're okay in that area. What do you want to do about interior work? How involved do you think Camille will want to be?"

For a moment Adam looked at Max strangely. Had he just called Camille by her first name? He didn't like the sound of her name on another man's lips, even if it was his cousin. It just sounded too intimate. But before he could make a foolish remark about it he took a deep steadying breath. "I'd like to keep her as involved as possible," he said slowly then looked around his desk for the magazines he'd been looking at earlier this morning.

"*You'd* like to keep her involved? I'm afraid to ask what that involvement would entail. But since I know you—" Max paused.

Adam ceased his search to glare at Max. "Let's keep our mind on business, shall we?"

Max chuckled. "If you can, I can."

"Here it is," Adam said and tossed the magazine in Max's direction. "I think contemporary Asian is a good way to go. With the large windows and open space it'll be a good contrast to the dated look it has now." That brought his thoughts back to something Camille had said to him. She'd once thought of the house as a castle. "The house has an old elegant feel. I'd like to keep that elegance but modernize it a bit."

Max flipped through the magazine.

"What do you think?" Adam asked.

"I think it's a good start. Antique on the outside and clean modern lines on the inside. It's good. I'll have Chanel call Camille in the morning to get her thoughts."

"I'll call her," Adam said quickly.

Max arched a brow. "Why?"

"Why what?"

Max set the magazine back onto the desk and relaxed in his chair. "Chanel is my assistant. She gets paid a tidy sum to make phone calls. Why can't she call Camille?"

"Because we agreed to keep her informed and to take her suggestions on this project. Chanel is used to making mundane calls. This will be detailed and in depth. Discussing decorating options isn't something your assistant should be handling."

"Adam," Max warned in a low tone.

Adam threw up his hands. "What?"

"This is business, remember."

"And I'm treating it as business," Adam argued.

"You personally took her to the airport today. You had dinner with her last night. Don't try to play innocent with me. I know you."

For a moment Adam was quiet, then he smiled. "You taught me most of what I know."

Max nodded his agreement. "And that's why I'm reminding you that this is business. Besides, she's not what you're used to. Leave her alone."

Adam didn't like Max's words but wasn't going to spend more time arguing the facts with him. "My dealings with Camille Davis are strictly business. I don't need you to remind me of that." He said the words and knew as he did that they were a lie.

"Excuse me, Adam?" Cindy, Adam's assistant buzzed through the intercom into his office.

"Yes?" Adam answered tersely.

"There's a call for you on line three."

"Take a message. I'm in a meeting."

Cindy cleared her throat. "Um, it's Kim Alvarez."

Silence filled the office. Max stared at Adam. Adam stared at the phone. Cindy had worked for Adam since the company's inception, and she'd known him all his life since they'd grown up as neighbors. So when she said his name again, this time very slowly, Adam realized this was serious.

"I'll take it."

The second Max left his office and closed the door Adam picked up the receiver and pressed the red blinking light to the line Kim was holding on.

"Adam Donovan," he said as if introductions were necessary.

"Hi, Adam."

Her voice was still smoky. Still as smooth as that drop of honey in a steamy cup of tea. Adam closed his eyes to the memory. "Hello, Kim."

They hadn't spoken in years, nine to be exact, and yet she affected him, in a way that he couldn't explain.

"How are you?"

Because he couldn't explain the effect she still had on him and because his mind was now criss-crossing between two women he didn't possess a lot of patience. "You call me after walking out of my life nine years ago to ask how I'm doing?" To his own ears he sounded wounded and if truth be told he still was. Kim had walked out of his life without a goodbye or explanation. He'd awakened one morning and she was gone, just like that. So while her voice still warmed him, he wouldn't act excited to hear from her.

"I'm calling because I needed to talk to you." She took a deep breath. "I know how long it's been just like I know you're probably still very angry with me. I'm asking for the chance to explain."

"Explanation time has expired. If you have something else you'd like to say I wish you'd make it quick. I was in a meeting."

"Don't be rude, Adam, it doesn't fit you."

"You have no idea what fits me. You don't know me." And he didn't know her. He'd never known her. For four years they'd dated, slept together, shared meals together, planned their future together and he didn't know her. About three months after she'd left he realized that and accepted it as his first major mistake.

Kim expelled a breath. "Adam, I'm just asking for a chance. We can go to lunch or dinner or something."

"Where are you?"

"I'm back in Vegas."

With his free hand Adam rubbed his eyes. "Why?"

"My family's here. You know that," she said with a hint of agitation.

"They were here when you left so don't fake the family values trip for me. How long will you be in town?"

"I think I'm staying."

Adam was quiet, not sure what to say or how to react to that announcement. He didn't care if Kim was back in Vegas or not and he damn sure didn't care if she was staying. She was a part of his past and she would never be considered anything else.

"That's fine if that's what you want, Kim. But as I said before, I don't need an explanation and I choose who I'll share my meals with." With bitter clarity he remembered the pain of those three months after she'd left and balled one hand into a fist. "I don't want to have lunch or dinner with you. I don't want to see you."

"You're being childish, Adam. What happened was a long time ago. Let me explain so we can move on."

"I've already moved on. Goodbye, Kim." He hung up the phone before she could speak another word.

Chapter 5

Camille scraped the bottom of the cup, licking the last portion of strawberry yogurt from the plastic spoon as she sat in her home office. Her stomach was far from full but she didn't have time for a debate. It was almost ten o'clock. In less than six hours the CK Davis Design fall line would be on display. She'd booked the Gold Room of the Millennium Hotel for this production. The total price tag including staff, lighting, sound and the after party was almost a million dollars.

But it was worth it.

The line was fabulous, if she could say so herself. Five evening gowns, six business suits, six casual ensembles and the twelve-outfit launch to her young adult line. It was risky she knew, combining a young adult line with her other ones, but she'd decided to take a chance. All of her regular buyers would be there as well as the ones in the young adult arena that had been sent special invitations. The prereviews raved, boasting about Teka Simmons's—the head of the young adult line—fresh, new designs.

All of this was great news, so why were her hands shaking and her head spinning with worst-case scenarios?

She reached for her glass of water and took a gulp. "Everything will be okay," she whispered to herself. She emptied the glass of water and waited for sweet relief. It did not come.

The shaking intensified until she felt as if she would fall out of her chair. Her heart hammered against her chest and she slapped her palms down on the blotter on her desk. With vicious determination Camille tried to get a hold of this situation. She did not have time for a breakdown. In one hour she was expected at the hotel. She needed to be dressed, have her hair and makeup done professionally and troubleshoot any and everything that could possibly go wrong with the show. She did not need to be on the brink of a nervous breakdown.

Her cell phone rang and she cursed the loud chirping. Snatching it from where it sat on the corner of the desk she flipped the top open and put it to her ear. "Ca…mille Davis," she attempted to say calmly.

"What's wrong?" Adam asked immediately.

Camille closed her eyes and groaned. In the last two weeks she'd spoken to Adam a couple of times, always pertaining to the house in some way. Not once in that time had Adam said anything alluding to the personal connection they'd shared when she was in Vegas, or that scorching kiss in the conference room at his office. After berating herself over the issue Camille had decided his business-only attitude was for the best.

But the last thing she needed right now was to have to talk to him.

"Nothing. You just caught me at a bad time," she said praying she sounded sane.

"Are you sitting down?"

"Yes," she said with confusion. "What do you want, Adam?"

"Sit back in your chair and close your eyes," he directed.

Camille swore then switched the phone to her other ear, her hands still shaking as she did. "I don't have time for this. The show is in a couple of hours and there are a million things I need to do."

"Sit back and close your eyes, Camille," Adam said sternly. "Take a few deep breaths."

She took a deep breath, then realized that as stubborn as Adam was he wasn't going to let her off the phone until she did what he said. Not in the mood for a tug-of-war with him she sat back in the chair and reluctantly closed her eyes.

"Breathe, Camille. Slowly, deeply. Just breathe," he chanted.

The first time she did what he said in an effort to speed up this conversation. The second time it was because it was easier. The third time was because she was beginning to feel a lot better.

"I was calling because one of the rooms on the second level is being demolished this weekend. The blueprints say it's a bedroom, a little girl's bedroom. I wanted to know before I got there if there was anything you wanted me to save for you. Maybe some old love letters, dirty magazines you once hid from your father, anything along those lines."

Despite her immense discomfort Camille gave a slight chuckle. "I've already been to the house and packed up the things that I want to keep. I left instructions with the moving company to pack everything else and put it into storage. So your demolition plans are okay."

"And the fashion show will be perfect," he said seriously.

She expelled a breath. Why, of all the people in the world, could Adam Donovan so effortlessly ease her fears?

"The designs are great," she said wistfully.

He chuckled. "You sound surprised."

"No, I'm not. But then that's just my opinion."

Camille cleared her throat. "Some of the prereviews said the same thing."

"I know. I've read them."

She sat straight up in her chair. "You did? Why? I mean, I didn't know you were interested in fashion." This was too comfortable. Talking to him as if they'd been friends for years, sharing things that she hadn't even fully acknowledged for herself.

"Why? Because I'm a man?" Adam laughed again. "I assure you I like to look good just like you do."

"Okay, I'm sure you don't need me to entertain you. And since I've answered your questions can I go now?" This easy rapport concerned her. The last thing she needed on today of all days was to have her mind muddled by thoughts of Adam and how much she wished she could see him instead of talk to him on the phone.

"Stay calm," he said slowly. "You've been preparing for this day for months. You've taken care of every detail right down to the font on the programs."

She smiled because she'd probably mentioned that to him in one of their many conversations over the last two weeks. And apparently he'd remembered.

Adam continued to speak. "I know this day is very important to you but it doesn't define you, Camille. You are a good person with or without a successful fashion line."

Her fingers were still shaking although her breathing was regulated now. She wasn't focusing so much on what could go wrong at the show this evening but on the sound of his voice. The deep timbre that filtered calm and acceptance through her soul. Her heart swelled and she almost sighed. Almost.

He was still Adam Donovan, her business partner until this deal was done. He lived in Las Vegas, hundreds of miles away from her. They were not involved and they were not friends. And this longing she had to get to know him better would have to stop.

"Thank you for saying that," she said finally. "I really need to get going if there's nothing else you need."

He was silent for a minute or so then said, "No, Camille. There's nothing else I need. Have a great day."

"Thanks," she mumbled and hurriedly disconnected the line. Dropping the phone on her desk she buried her face in her hands.

The walls of the Gold Room were draped in dark chocolate satin and columns lined the walkway separating the first rows of seats from where the models would be on display. Gold chandeliers sparkled while a fantastic light show glittered throughout the room. Music blared through the overhead speakers casting a partylike mood on everyone in the room.

From what Camille had been told the early arrivers were enjoying themselves, indulging in the unlimited wine and cheese displays strategically placed throughout the ballroom.

Backstage was a different story entirely. There were at least a hundred people crammed into the small space. Vanities lined one wall where models sat and make-up artists stood. Racks carrying clothes were pushed up and down while half-naked models struggled to find the right outfit, the perfect wig or corresponding shoes. Including herself, Dana and Sofari they had ten other assistants, the choreographer and the site supervisor so they should have been rolling easy. And they probably were, but Camille was again a nervous wreck.

However, she wasn't in danger of fainting this time. Not that anyone would notice what with all the people backstage. Her mind kept drifting back to the phone call this morning, to the man that had surprised her with his kind words.

"Okay, I don't want you to panic," Dana began when she approached Camille.

Camille, who had been loving her little daydream, was thrust back to reality with Dana's excited voice. From the way her eyes were dancing Camille presumed that whatever she had to say was a good thing. "Okay, what am I not panicking about?"

Dana stepped to the side revealing a line of four mouthwateringly handsome men and one beautiful woman.

"I know their names weren't on the guest list but I didn't think you'd want me to turn them away," Dana said with a smile that a blind man could see.

Camille knew exactly what her friend was thinking but couldn't focus on that. Her gaze had been captured and held firmly by the man with warm brown eyes and caramel toned skin.

She couldn't believe he was here, in L.A., at her fashion show. She smiled then felt her legs about to give way and remembered to breathe. "Ah, no. Of course we wouldn't turn them away," she said with a shaky voice.

He took a step closer and reached for her hand. "I didn't want you to be alone today."

"Adam." His name came out in a whisper and she tried to contain the tears forming in her eyes.

He squeezed her hand then turned towards the other people with him. "Let me introduce you," he began. "This is my brother, Trent, and this is my oldest brother, Linc, and his wife Jade. And of course, you remember Max."

Camille felt a bit overwhelmed. These were four of the best-looking men she'd ever seen in her life. From their well-built frames to their totally masculine aura they were the epitome of fine black men. She swallowed hard and focused on the woman who had the privilege of being married to one of them. "It's a pleasure to meet you all." She prayed she didn't sound goofy but couldn't think of anything else to say.

"The pleasure is ours," Jade said. "Now since we're the intruders we'll just go grab a seat and get out of your hair. You've definitely got your hands full back here."

"Yes, it is a madhouse," Camille responded, pleased with the down-to-earth way Jade had spoken. Camille was always uncomfortable meeting new people and meetings with beautiful women were definitely difficult situations. You would think that she'd be used to it by now but she tended to consider the models, both men and women, as employees and never really worried about whether or not they liked her.

Jade Donovan was giving her a brilliant smile through kind eyes and Camille appreciated it, immensely.

"I agree with Jade. I'm going to find a seat," Max said then gave Camille a nod. "Knock 'em dead."

Linc grabbed his wife's hand and said, "I expect you're about to give my wife a lot of reasons to dig into my pocket. But if it'll make her happy, I appreciate it."

Camille smiled when Jade elbowed him in the ribs. "Thanks. I think."

Trent eyed her closely and Camille felt a moment's apprehension. He was taller than his brothers and his cousin, probably somewhere near six feet four inches. His complexion was a shade darker than Adam's but not as dark as Linc's. His eyes were brown and not soft but not quite hard, either. He watched her as if he expected her to grow another head or perhaps puke pea soup.

Adam's grip tightened on her hand. "Trent you should go and get a seat, too," he said.

Trent nodded then extended his hand to her. Camille looked from Adam and then back to Trent, unsure of what she should do. Beside her Dana nudged her. With her free hand she grasped Trent's and looked up at him as he spoke.

"I like your designs. I'm sure it'll be a great show."

Boy, it looked as if those words had been wrenched from him with the terseness in which he spoke. She nodded and again mumbled, "Thank you."

"Sorry about that," Adam said immediately after Trent had walked through the curtains that would take him to the seats. "He's not usually so intense. Well, actually he is, but I warned him to take it easy on you."

He'd turned to face her and was rubbing his hands up and down her arms. This should have bothered her but instead it relaxed her. Camille really needed to get a grip on how that made her feel.

"I don't understand. What are you doing here?" she asked when she could think beyond the fact that he was touching her in a way that was far too intimate to be friendly.

"Camille! You've gotta come quick there's a problem with the models!" A very out of breath Sofari came running up to her.

Camille turned out of Adam's grasp and faced her assistant. "What problem?"

Sofari looked from her to Adam then back to Camille. "You should come with me. I can show you better than I can tell you."

"Fine," Camille snapped, then turned back to Adam.

She opened her mouth to speak but he silenced her with a look. "Go. I'll be waiting for you after the show."

She nodded and hurried away.

Adam was about to walk away when he felt a hand on his arm. "She doesn't know why you came, but I do," Dana said.

"Excuse me?"

"You don't remember me, do you?" she asked as she leaned against the wall.

Adam lifted a brow. "Should I?"

"I was with Camille at the Gramercy the first time she met you."

Adam nodded as if he remembered.

"I told her that night she should have left with you. I can't believe she ran into you again and that now you two are working together. It must be fate."

She smiled as she said the last words but was walking away before he could ask her to elaborate. He did remember the woman, although her hair was shorter now. She and Camille had been sitting at the bar when he'd come in for a drink the day after the wedding.

Fate.

Adam let the word swirl around in his mind.

Whatever it was that brought him and Camille together he wouldn't think about complaining. After all, he had dropped everything to come to L.A. for a fashion show because he felt she needed him. Okay, he wasn't totally self-centered so he didn't for one minute believe that it was him personally that she needed. She just needed someone who was in her corner and someone who wouldn't hesitate to let her know that.

His mistake had been calling Linc to ensure the availability of the family's private jet in order to get to L.A. on time. That request had Linc asking questions, which had ultimately led to Jade's questions, which ended with all of them climbing into the jet to meet the infamous C.K. Davis.

It didn't matter. The only thing he was concerned with was the look of pleasant surprise on Camille's face when they appeared. He wanted to capture that look, to bottle it and keep it especially for himself. All around him was a flurry of activity, so much so that he was thrust back into reality and the fact that the fashion show would be starting in a few minutes.

He'd just taken a step to go through the curtain and find a seat with his family when again he felt a hand on his arm.

"You've got to help us," she said desperately.

"What are you talking about now?" Adam turned and asked the woman he'd just been speaking to. "And what's your name?"

"Sorry, I'm Dana. Camille's best friend and partner. But that's neither here nor there." Grabbing him by the hand she began pulling Adam farther toward the back.

"Wait a minute. Dana? Where are we going? Is something wrong with Camille?" That thought had his stomach plummeting.

Dana stopped walking and turned to him. "Camille is currently about to hyperventilate as a result of the agency not sending the number of male models we requested. So I need you to change and get ready to go on stage."

"What?" Adam yelled and remained rooted where he stood. "I'm not a model."

"No." Dana looked him up and down. "Not by trade, but you certainly could be. Anyway, we need you. Camille needs you."

Why did Adam get the distinct impression that Dana knew by putting it that way he'd have no choice but to do what she asked? "This is insane." He cursed. "Where is she?"

"There's not enough time," Dana began saying.

"I'm not doing this until I talk to her. Where is she?"

Dana sighed. "Okay, she's at the end of the hall but hurry up—you're going on in the second set.

And don't tell her that you're doing it or she'll get even more upset."

Stomping away Adam realized the truth in Dana's words. Camille wouldn't want to feel like she was imposing on him or anyone else in any way. So he wouldn't tell her that he was about to make a humongous fool of himself to save her show.

He found her sitting in a chair, her legs spread, while some skinny man with hair too primped to be masculine pushed her head between her legs. Her entire body trembled and Adam wanted to yell for the man to stop pushing her face into the floor but held tight to his rage. Instead he simply scooped her up out of the chair and took a seat himself, planting her firmly on his lap.

"Oh, my," the skinny guy said as he fanned himself.

"Get lost," Adam demanded.

"Adam…it's…such…a…mess," Camille hissed.

"All right, baby, just calm down. It's going to be okay." He began massaging her back, making big lazy circles until her breathing almost returned to normal. "Now, tell me what's bothering you."

She swallowed and clenched her hands together. "I… We needed six male models. They only sent… four."

"But your line consists of mostly women's attire. Can't one of the men just double up?"

She nodded affirmatively. "That would work for all of the scenes except one when all of them are needed on the floor at one time. There's no way I can get more models at this point. That means I'll have to pull two outfits."

Her breathing increased and he rubbed her back faster. "No. You won't. Don't worry. I'll take care of it."

"How? Do you have models in your pocket?"

Adam smiled. She was coming around. He kissed her forehead. "No, I don't have models in my pocket but I don't like seeing you upset. Do me a favor and take your place over there. Look pretty and smile for the cameras. I'll handle the rest."

He stood and placed her on her feet. She was about to question him and he raised a brow. She waved a hand. "Forget it. You're stubborn and arrogant enough to argue with whatever I say."

"You're absolutely right, so go over there and take your place."

Astonishingly, she did as he said and he made a beeline for the curtain and out into the audience to where his family sat. Calculating as he walked he configured who would be the easiest one to recruit. None of the Donovan men would be easy to coerce in this matter so on impulse he grabbed Trent's arm and hauled him up. "Come with me."

"What the hell are you doing? The show's about to start," Trent protested until they were again backstage.

"Look, I need you to do this without all the questions and hoopla. She's in a bind and she needs our help." He looked Trent up and down and sighed. "I hope she has something that fits you."

"You hope who has something that fits? Are you losing your mind?" Trent asked.

"Great! You're both here. Dana said to bring you these." A tall honey-toned woman handed them two suits.

Adam took them from her hands without another thought but Trent continued to stare.

"Thanks," Adam said.

"No problem. One of you will be walking with me in about ten minutes so can you hurry it up," she said then turned and walked away.

Trent clapped a hand on Adam's shoulder. "Tell me what I'm thinking is wrong and that you're not about to ask me to be a model. And then tell me her name and number," he said, referring to the beauty who'd just given them suits.

Adam thrust a suit into Trent's chest. "You're out of luck because I can't tell you either of those things."

Trent growled and pushed the suit away. "I'm not doing it."

"C'mon, man. She needs our help."

Adam had already started walking towards one of the changing areas. Trent reluctantly followed. "No, she needs a professional model, which we are not. And why are you so intent on helping her?"

Adam was already stripping off his shirt. "You asked me that already."

Trent reached for the buttons on his shirt. "And you didn't answer me. Why is she so important to you? It's just a business deal. This fashion show has nothing to do with you."

Adam knew Trent's words were right and he couldn't readily explain it, but the only thing that mattered to him, again, was Camille. If this fashion show wasn't a success or didn't go off in any way she'd be devastated. And while he knew that in business things didn't always go exactly the way you wanted, he suspected that Camille would take this setback a lot harder than your average person. He didn't want her to go through that.

"Do me a favor and just get into that suit. All we have to do is walk out there and walk back. We're not selling our souls."

Trent frowned. "No, I'm not. But you're going to owe me big-time for this."

Adam didn't smile and he didn't feel relief. Owing Trent was never a good thing. "Fine, whatever you want."

"I want her name and number," Trent said as he took the jacket off the hanger and slipped it on.

From backstage Camille watched the show begin. The lights were fantastic, the music on point and the crowd excited by them both. Her heart pounded in her chest but she didn't feel like its thumping was strangling her. Instead she felt motivated, rejuvenated.

The models owned the catwalk; with attitude and flare only seasoned professionals possessed they displayed her designs in a way that had cameras flashing and the crowd applauding.

A quick glance to the first row on the right and she spotted the Donovans. Linc and his wife were all smiles as she pointed to various outfits. He had one arm around her and nodded as she talked enthusiastically. He loved her, that much was obvious. Camille wondered how that felt. Jade looked as if she owned the world. It wasn't the designer clothes she wore or the flawless makeup and stylishly coiffed hair that Camille envied. It was the sheer self-confidence the woman exuded. She knew exactly who she was and what her purpose in the world was. More importantly, she had someone who loved her.

Pulling her gaze away from the couple because it made her sad she looked at Max, who appeared enchanted by the parade of women. His light-colored eyes glistened as he nodded his own approval of the floor-length lavender sheath. Camille smiled proudly a second before noticing that two of the Donovans were missing. She was about to scan the crowd for them when the music changed.

She knew this scene, knew that it was missing two key players and tried not to focus on that fact.

Adam said he would take care of it. She hadn't bothered to ask him how, she'd just trusted that he would. That in itself was strange because Camille didn't readily trust anyone.

Dana came to stand behind her, placing a hand on her shoulder. "It's going well," she said encouragingly.

"So far," Camille said keeping her eyes on the stage.

The first couple wore white, the woman a tea-length satin halter dress with a sparkling diamond broach. The man in a white suit with satin lapels and diamond-trimmed sleeves. The next couple... Camille gasped.

Tia St. Martin, one of the most requested runway models in the United States, stepped out first, her black dress clinging to her sleek body. Tia was five feet eleven inches of honey-brown beauty. Her eyes were hazel, her cheekbones high, her lips small and pouty. Her hair was long, golden strands hanging past her shoulders, today held back by black diamond-encrusted clips. A sheer wrap went with the dress and she held it aloof in her right hand so that it dragged behind her. Suddenly the end of the wrap was lifted and the man appeared.

The suit fit Trent Donovan well, although it could have been a bit longer in the arms. Then again, she hadn't been prepared for a larger-than-life male model. Still, the black looked good on him. His shirt and tie were black as well, the only thing adding light to his ensemble was the diamond cufflinks. He followed behind the woman in a smooth, confident swagger. The crowd loved it.

Tia took long strides down the walkway while Trent walked behind her watching—more like gawking—at the sway of her hips in the tight dress. Tia paused, spread her legs and struck a pose. A trained male model would have paused beside her, struck a pose and allowed the audience to take in their attire. Trent, however, slipped a hand around her waist and pulled her to him. Tia didn't act surprised but went willingly into his arms so that the entire move looked orchestrated. Applause echoed throughout the room as they turned and walked back through the curtain.

Tia and Dana exchanged a look, then gave in to laughter. "That couldn't have gone better if we'd planned it," Camille admitted.

Dana agreed. "He is beyond fine. We should definitely think about hiring him for the catalog."

"I doubt if he'll do it. I can't imagine how he was ever coerced into getting out there today. Modeling does not look like Trent Donovan's cup of tea," Camille was saying when she could swear her eyes were deceiving her.

He was sexy in the tuxedo she'd first seen him in and even sexier in the slacks and collarless shirt he'd worn into the bar that night. On this last trip to Vegas he'd worn a suit both days, and she'd admired his physique over and over again. Tonight he didn't just wear a suit, he wore *her* suit. She remembered drawing the lines, angling the cut and deciding on the fabric. This was her favorite of the collection, its dark brown hue perfectly accenting the female's cream crepe strapless dress.

He did not walk behind the woman. Adam Donovan demanded a more upfront role. He came out first, the female model holding his hand and trailing a step behind him. He had his other hand in his pocket opening the jacket so that his cream-striped brown shirt was on display. The shirt fit him well, so well her mouth watered at the perfectly defined pectorals and tapered waist.

They reached the end of the runway and the female model released his hand and pressed her body close to his side, her face angled so that it appeared she was resting her head on his shoulder. Adam stared forward, as if the female wasn't even there. Slipping his hand from his pocket he executed a turn and the woman followed.

Camille's breath lodged somewhere between her lungs and her throat as flashes from the camera and the illumination from the light show sparkled and dazzled against the dark backdrop and she watched Adam's long strides eat up the runway. He was confident, arrogant and gorgeous. Heat pooled between her legs and she couldn't take her eyes off of him.

He looked serious, like this was taking a lot of concentration on his part; then his gaze caught hers and that serious expression vanished. He smiled and her legs buckled.

"Damn, Camille. If you don't do him I'm going to hell for cheating on Carl," Dana whispered.

Camille heard her words and imagined doing just that. She loved that suit on him but couldn't help thinking of him without it. Naked and amenable to whatever she desired was how she now envisioned Adam. In her bed or his, it didn't really matter as long as he was there.

Chapter 6

The crowd went nuts clapping and the music seemed just a bit louder when Adam and the model exited the stage. Camille had planned to run to him, to thank him profusely for what he'd done but her feet weren't cooperating. She seemed glued to that spot, her mind replaying how he'd gotten up in front of all those people, for her.

Dana, pulling on the sleeve of her blouse, snapped her out of her reverie and Camille looked up to see Adam standing in front of her. He wore a huge grin that managed to make him look ten times sexier than when he was serious on the catwalk.

"So how was my debut?" he asked in that casual air of his.

Camille didn't know what to say so she hugged him instead. "Thank you, so much," she whispered.

For a split second he didn't touch her and Camille thought she'd stepped over the line. But then his arms encircled her waist, his hands moving slowly up her back, spreading heat throughout her on their journey. He held her tightly and Camille imagined that this was more than a thank-you, more than a friendly gesture of appreciation.

Before she could romanticize the moment any longer Camille pulled away, smiling nervously. "You were really good. If I didn't know any better I'd swear you've done that before."

Adam still touched her, one hand possessively remaining around her waist. He lifted a finger to her chin and simply stared at her. Camille couldn't quite describe what she was feeling at that point. His gaze was intense as if there was something he wanted to say.

"You're feeling better," he said softly.

She nodded. "Yes. I'm feeling a lot better."

"Camille, the kids are on," Dana announced, effectively breaking the trance between her and Adam.

Camille attempted to move away from him to return to her spot where she could watch the show. He didn't let her go like she'd anticipated, but stood beside her taking her hand in his. She didn't even think to argue because it felt so right.

Together they watched the group of teenagers in stylish outfits designed for their thicker frames and fuller figures. It was incredible to see their eyes alight with the appreciation of the audience. One girl in particular, Evanna, who was sixteen and wore a woman's size fourteen, had been extremely nervous about today's show. Camille had spent endless hours with her, going to lunch or to a movie or just hanging out. She saw so much of herself in Evanna that she tried to give her everything that her own childhood was missing.

Evanna wore black capris with gold stitching and a gold tank top with a sheer covering that didn't draw your attention to her large breasts or her plump behind. Instead, the black trimmed her figure, drawing attention to her five-foot-seven-inch height and long legs. She was a very pretty girl with a bright future ahead of her and Camille didn't want to see it hampered by low self-esteem and doubts.

For the second time today her heart swelled until she thought tears were inevitable. She took deep, steadying breaths because the last thing she wanted was for Adam to see her breaking down again. He probably already thought she was a basket case.

"She looks really good," Dana commented.

Camille nodded. "She does."

Adam heard the pride in her voice and wondered

again about the woman inside. Originally he'd
thought she was timid and a little jittery, then he'd
seen her with her stepmother and felt the tension
between them. But that wasn't abnormal now he
was looking at her differently, watching her watch
the young girl on the runway as if, in some way, she
wished it were her.

Had she wanted to be a model and for some
reason didn't try? Again, he thought of her stepmother and how great a possibility that was. That
would explain a lot about her: the reluctance to act,
the fear of not pleasing everyone.

Inadvertently he tightened his grip on her hand
as thoughts of protecting her against all odds took
over. She looked up at him in question and he
smiled, rubbing his thumb over her fingers instead
of squeezing them tightly.

In his mind it just wasn't possible that she
couldn't see how beautiful and talented she was but
then he was very aware of the dangers of low self-
esteem. A girl he went to college with had succumbed to the stress of not feeling pretty enough
or skinny enough. She'd died after months in the
hospital, suffering pitifully at the hands of anorexia.
Fear clutched his heart as he considered how dangerous this could be if Camille were suffering this
way. He vowed to find out as soon as the show was
over. And while he doubted Camille would be completely forthcoming with him, he had a sneaky suspicion that his best ally was standing very close. He

eyed Dana and made a mental note to get her alone at the first available opportunity.

The show was a rousing success. Everyone said so, from the reporters to the photographers and even the impromptu models.

"My modeling days are over," Trent said adamantly as they took their seats at the head table during the after party. "It doesn't pay well," he added, eyeing Adam.

"I am not asking for her number to give to my big brother. Besides, you had your hands all over her onstage, I would think you'd have gotten all her vital statistics by now."

Linc and Max laughed with Adam as Trent's frown increased. "No. I didn't get her vital statistics, but I certainly plan to," he said.

Camille interrupted. "If you're talking about Tia St. Martin, I can put you in touch with her agent."

Trent looked at her and visibly relaxed. "That's okay. I'll find her."

Adam watched as he looked across the room where a group of models had convened. He quickly spotted the tall beauty that had captured his brother's attention and shook his head. That was one battle he did not envy being a part of.

"Camille, I've ordered several gowns from the catalog and that sexy little cream outfit the model walking with Adam had on. How long will it take for delivery?" Jade asked.

"Thanks, Jade. I'll call the factory first thing Monday morning and have them do an overnight shipment."

"Don't thank me, it's a worthy investment. You are truly a fashion diva. My mother-in-law is going to be sorry she missed the opportunity to meet you."

Jade's words struck a chord with Adam. He hadn't thought of Camille in his personal space but here she was sitting at the head of a table filled with his family and they seemed to like her. However, his parents were a different story entirely. Not that they were bad people; Henry and Beverly Donovan were loving parents and compassionate people. Their forty-year marriage had even made them blissful romantics. They would like Camille, he finally decided.

"So how's the house coming along?" Linc was asking when Adam had tuned back in to the conversation at hand.

"Demolition started today," Max said. "That'll take the next two to three weeks, then we'll be ready to start with the decorating."

Linc nodded and took a sip of his wine. "Has Sal already starting shopping?"

Salvatore Gianni was the president of Gianni Concepts, one of the top interior designers on the west coast. Adam used him for almost all of his projects. "He left yesterday for India," Adam answered.

Camille looked surprised. "India?"

"I thought you discussed the décor with her, Adam." Max sounded alarmed.

"Oh, he did," Camille spoke up. "I just didn't realize that someone would be traveling so far to simply decorate a house."

"We want the best and Sal knows where to find it. Don't worry, it'll be great," Adam said placing a hand over hers.

"I'm not worried," she said. "I trust your judgment."

Wow. Adam felt as if he'd been struck by lightning. Had she said she trusted him? No, what she'd said was that she trusted his judgment, in terms of decorating the house. That was it. What else was he hoping for?

"Well, well, well, don't we look quite cozy?" Moreen said as she made her way closer to Camille.

Adam saw the moment Mrs. Davis's voice registered with Camille. Her eyes, which had been dancing with remnants of excitement from the successful show, darkened. Her chin, which had been held high, fell. She looked up to see her stepmother and had to force a smile. "Hello, Moreen."

Moreen rolled her eyes. "Sit up straight, Camille. I swear you'd think I never taught you anything."

Then Moreen's gaze shifted to Adam and her smile brightened. "Mr. Donovan, it's a pleasure and a surprise to see you here. I didn't know that fashion was your thing."

Having witnessed this switch in demeanor before, Adam quickly stood and reached for Mrs. Davis's hand. "It's nice to see you again as well, Mrs. Davis."

"Oh my, where are my manners? For a moment there I was acting as sheepish as Camille." She spoke quickly and stepped to the side. "This is my date for the evening, Carl Rabodi. I'm sure you've all heard of him."

If it were possible Camille's shoulders slumped even farther but she held her head up high now, her eyes the only giveaway to the anger within.

"Fashions by Rabodi," Jade said quickly. "Of course we know who you are. Your fall show is next week, right?"

"Skulking for ideas, Carl?" Dana quipped.

Carl Rabodi, a man of at least thirty-five years, stood tall, his dark hair slicked back and shining. The sprays of gray at his temples gave him an almost distinguished air. He smiled and nodded in Dana's direction. "No, my dear. My show is ready. But I must say that I thoroughly enjoyed myself at your show and thank Moreen so much for inviting me."

"Nonsense, Carl. Camille should be flattered that such an esteemed designer as yourself would take the time to come to her little show at all," Moreen said with disdain.

"CK Davis Designs is a very reputable fashion house. One Mr. Rabodi might want to keep an eye on in the future. I know that as far as I'm concerned, the bulk of my wardrobe will come from her," Jade added absently.

Linc followed her lead. "Her men's line was notable. I'm actually toying with the idea of having her exclusively at the Gramercy's boutique."

Carl cleared his throat. "You own boutiques, sir? I would be happy to schedule a private showing of Rabodi Fashions for your consideration."

"My brother owns the Gramercy Casino and Resort in Las Vegas," Adam offered. "And his wife has a very reputable spa and salon. By adding CK Davis Designs to their business ventures their success will only multiply."

"Then they should definitely speak with you, Carl. You've so much more experience in this area than Camille."

"Yes, I'd really like a private meeting with you, ah…"

"Donavan," Linc supplied. "I'm Lincoln Donovan and this is my wife, Jade. You can call my office on Monday and have my assistant check my schedule but tonight has sort of sealed the deal with CK Davis Designs. Maybe another opportunity for your company will arise."

Moreen looked as if her eyes would bulge right out of their sockets. Dana sipped from her glass to cover a chuckle.

"Camille, I'd like a status on the house when you've finished celebrating your little triumph tonight." Moreen fairly spat the words.

Adam was about to speak but this time was silenced by a look from Camille. "If you'd like a status, Moreen, you should probably call Mr. Donovan's office. I don't deal in the daily workings of the project."

Moreen was promptly surprised by Camille's retort but carefully disguised it. "I just thought since you seem to be making a habit of sitting under him that you'd have some clue as to what was going on with the property. But I should have known you wouldn't be that tuned to your business investments."

"To the contrary, I know what he's doing and when he will be doing it. But I have a business of my own to run, therefore I can't be expected to keep you in the loop." This time Camille spoke sweetly before lifting her glass of champagne that had just been poured by the waiter who arrived sometime during the exchange. "I propose a toast," she began and waited while the others at the table lifted their glasses in salute. "To CK Davis Designs and the new fall line."

"To Camille Davis and her talented designs," Adam added.

"Hear, hear," Jade chimed.

Moreen could only huff before grabbing Carl's hand and stalking off.

Adam couldn't resist. He leaned over and kissed Camille's cheek. "Well done," he whispered and was rewarded by a sparkling smile.

* * *

"I don't think I'm going to sleep a wink tonight," Camille said as she crossed the threshold into her apartment.

Adam had accompanied her home and was now taking her key out of the door and closing it soundly behind him. It was after midnight and she was feeling very relaxed and just a tad tipsy after all the champagne she'd indulged in this evening. But after Moreen's arrival and departure she felt the need to do something out of the ordinary.

At first she couldn't believe that Moreen had showed up and with her biggest competitor at that. But then she realized that was precisely what could be expected from her wonderful stepmother. The moment Moreen arrived she'd felt as if the floor was going to swallow her up. Then she'd looked over and saw Adam, noticing that he touched her hand. Jade and Linc had even come to her rescue. Camille figured that if these people that she barely knew could stand up for her she damn sure better stand up for herself. So she'd said what needed to be said to Moreen and proceeded to party for the duration of the evening.

That decision was going to be hell to deal with in a few hours when the sun rose again, but she didn't care. She felt good right now and that's all that mattered.

"I could read you a bedtime story," Adam offered.

She turned, remembering that he was in her apartment with her and smiled slowly. Damn, he was one fine-ass black man. Her fingers actually itched to yank his shirt open and rub along the taut skin of his chest. Did champagne normally make her horny? She had no idea.

"You know bedtime stories?" she asked coyly and dropped her purse on the table. She was on her way to the couch when she stumbled. And of course, he caught her. She couldn't have planned it better if she were a romance writer.

His arms snaked around her waist, pulling her backside up against his front. Her entire world tilted. Now that could be another effect of too much champagne but she was betting it was too much Adam.

"I know a lot of things," he said, his mouth close to her ear. "For starters I know that you don't hold your liquor well." He moved them over to the couch and sat them both down.

"What?" she asked, letting her head fall back against the chair. "I've got a really good retort to that comment and just as soon as the room stops spinning I'm going to say it."

Adam chuckled and brushed her hair back from her forehead. "You had a good time tonight. I'm glad."

Camille let out a deep breath. "I did."

"You don't do that often, do you?"

He was lifting her legs onto his. She remembered this position from the hotel in Vegas and wanted to sigh. He was a man, alone with her in her apartment after a night of drinking and dancing. There were so many things he could be doing to her, things she probably wouldn't be disagreeable to, but he was taking off her shoes, rubbing her feet. She shifted until she was lying down, her head on the arm of the sofa. "I don't have a lot of time to relax and enjoy myself."

He moved to the other foot. "You should make the time. Linc used to have that same problem. I used to tell him repeatedly, business is good, money is even better, but happiness and fulfillment in your life is worth so much more."

Camille lifted her head slightly. "How old are you again?"

"It's not about age. It's about priorities and living a long and prosperous life. Business can't sustain you forever."

"And this is coming from a multimillionaire real estate mogul."

Adam smiled. "Yes, it is. Because besides all that, I know how to have fun and enjoy myself."

"Are you enjoying yourself now?" she asked because she most definitely was. His hands had traveled from her feet to her ankles and from her ankles to her calves. Her body was on fire as she anticipated his hands moving further north.

"I am."

His voice had lowered an octave and the room's

temperature increased. For one brief moment reality reared its ugly head and she remembered who she was, what she looked like, what size she wore and how none of that fit the type of woman Adam Donovan was used to. But then his hands were on her knees and suddenly none of that other stuff mattered.

"I'm having a very good time. How about you, Camille? Do you like when I touch you?"

She whispered yes and tried to keep from begging him to do so with a little more urgency.

Adam leaned forward and touched her lips lightly with his. Camille instantly grabbed his head, pulling him into a hot exchange of tongues, lips and teeth. His hands moved up until they were on her thighs and she quivered. He'd shifted until he was on top of her, his hands slipping deeper between her legs. She struggled to spread her legs so that he wouldn't encounter the part of her thighs that rubbed together and that's when it hit her…reality has that way of coming back with a vengeance.

She pulled away and struggled to get off the couch without tumbling to the floor. "I'm…ah… sorry," she murmured while trying to fix her clothes.

Adam sat up slowly then rested his elbows on his knees as he watched her begin to pace. "What's wrong, Camille? I thought you said you were having a good time."

"I was." She threw her hands up in the air. "I mean,

I had a great time at the party and I really appreciate you coming through at the fashion show. I just—"

She turned abruptly and bumped into him. He caught her by the shoulders. "You just what?"

"I'm not... I can't be what...um..." She couldn't think straight. So much had happened in the last twenty-four hours, her emotions had been on a roller coaster from the moment she woke up this morning. Add that to all the champagne she'd consumed and it was no wonder she didn't know if she were coming or going. "I'm drunk."

Adam grasped her nape and pulled her closer. "You're not quite drunk, just very, very relaxed. So I don't understand why you're pacing as if something upset you. Did I do something wrong?"

Camille shook her head negatively.

"Then tell me what the problem is, Camille."

"We're business associates," she said meekly.

It was Adam's turn to shake his head. "You've gotta come better than that, Camille. This has nothing to do with our business together. And everything to do with me and you."

She slipped out of his grasp. "There is no me and you."

Adam pushed his hands into his pockets. "So what do you call what just happened on that couch?"

"I don't know, physics. Or maybe we both had too much to drink or maybe it's just the momentum of the night. I don't know, Adam." She sighed. "I just know that this can't go any further."

"Why?"

"It just can't, okay?"

"No, it's not okay!" he roared.

She took a step back, not sure how to take his outburst.

Adam moved closer, reaching out a hand to touch her but she moved away again. "I'm sorry. I didn't mean to yell. It's just that it's frustrating trying to figure out what's wrong with you all the time. Why can't you just tell me what's bothering you so we can figure it out together? That's what adults do, Camille."

He was so right. He was so handsome and so perfect and he was so way out of her league. "You're right," she admitted. "I can't do this because I know that it's not what you really want."

He stared at her incredulously. "Come again?"

Adam had no idea how hard this was for her. It was one thing to know her limitations, to be forced to live with them her whole life. It was something else entirely to admit them to someone else. Especially someone like him.

"I know that I'm not the type of woman you usually go for. And I can't change that. As a matter of fact, I don't want to change it. I'm…I'm okay with who I am. And I don't do one-night stands. So it's best if you just go and we just concentrate on our business together from this point on." Damn, that hurt more than she'd imagined.

Adam didn't know what to say or do. He'd yelled at her once and she'd almost jumped out of her skin.

He'd never been a bully and didn't intend to start now. But that didn't stop the boiling rage simmering inside of him. "You have no idea what type of woman I go for," he said through clenched teeth. Damn, but he was tired of people assuming they knew him. Most of the time it was just the press printing their lies to sell more papers or magazines but he'd learned how to brush that off. Generally women had preconceived ideas about who he was and what he wanted but he'd never let that bother him, never cared because he knew their time was limited. But this time, this woman... He was outraged.

"Adam," she began.

"No. Don't say another word. I'm a grown man and I know who and what I want. I don't have a type or a particular brand in mind when I look for a woman. I tend to look for someone I enjoy spending time with. But I guess that's just beyond what my personality profile told you."

He was the one pacing now, unable to stop the incessant movement for fear of what he'd do if he was forced to stand still. "I didn't prejudge you, Camille, and I'm pissed off that you would do something like that to me."

"I didn't prejudge you. It's common knowledge. You're a rich, handsome, eligible bachelor. You enjoy women. Do you deny that?"

"No, I don't but—"

She cut him off. "There's no but. I know that I'm not slim and trim and sexy in a bikini. I know that

I'm probably not as outgoing as the other women you've dated and that's how I came to the conclusion that I wasn't your type. So that wasn't any prejudgment. That was just dealing with the facts."

"You are not that shallow. I know you're not."

"I am what I am, Adam. And therein lies the problem," she said simply and moved toward the door.

He opened his mouth to say something but she stopped him by opening the door and muttering, "Good night, Adam."

Because he had enough discipline to know when he'd reached his limit Adam moved toward the door, determined not to say another word or even look at her again for fear of blowing up completely. But he did stop in front of her. He kept his gaze forward as he took a deep breath, her scent permanently embedding itself in his mind. "You underestimate yourself and you underestimate me."

Chapter 7

Camille lay in her bed, eyes closed, covers drawn to her chest, unable to sleep. Upon Adam's departure she'd felt like crying, then she'd thought better of that useless pastime and resorted to anger. Tossing her clothes into a corner of her room, yanking her sheets down, then thrusting herself onto the mattress while her heart hammered in her chest.

He was an idiot if he couldn't see the obvious. But was she an even bigger idiot for pointing it out to him? What woman in her right mind turned Adam Donovan away? Well, she'd never professed to being in her right mind.

Instead she'd resigned herself to her fate and tossed and turned for the next hour or so hoping that morning would hurry up and come to give her a reason to put this dreadful night behind her.

On her nightstand the phone rang and she jumped. It was almost three in the morning. She rolled over and grabbed the phone before its shrill ringing could sound again. "Hello?"

"I want to apologize."

Camille sank back against her pillows, not believing the voice she was hearing on the other end. "Adam?"

"I shouldn't have gotten upset and I shouldn't have tried to push you to do something you obviously weren't ready for. I wasn't raised that way," he said quietly.

"Where are you?"

"I'm at a hotel."

There was a moment of silence, which Camille desperately wanted to fill. "Adam, I guess I was a bit out of line in the way I said what I needed to say. But it doesn't stop it from being true."

"Look, I can't tell you what to believe. I can only attest to what I know is true for me. I don't look for skinny women who look good in a bikini." He gave a wry chuckle. "I'm not saying I'm opposed to them, but they are not a prerequisite in my book.

"I like smart women, independent women and women who understand my warped sense of humor," he continued.

"You have a sense of humor?"

"My point exactly." He sighed. "I know that we are business partners but there's something more going on between us. I'm sure you know that already and I can't force you to act on it. But don't let your excuse for pushing me away be something as ludicrous as you not being my type. Because if I did have a type—" he paused "—you would undoubtedly be it."

Camille didn't know what to say. She didn't know what to believe. He didn't have to call her. He could have gone to his hotel and gone to bed. He could return to Las Vegas and never give her another thought, outside of the house deal. So why was he calling her? Why was he telling her all this?

"I've always wondered what it felt like to be svelte and tall and thin like the rest of the models I employ. They look so happy when they slip into the beautiful clothes and smile for the cameras."

"Don't be fooled, they're not happy. They're hungry."

Camille laughed.

"I'm serious. I dated a model before and she starved herself to the point that I was sick for her. The grass isn't always greener on the other side, Camille. Besides, you're beautiful just as you are. And for the record, you're not a day away from obesity so stop acting that way."

"You don't understand," she tried to say.

"I understand that society puts a lot of pressure

on women to be a certain size, a certain look. I understand that as a woman in the fashion industry you would want to concede to those standards. It's just not necessary. I like you just the way you are, just as I'm sure a lot of other people do. But none of that means anything if you don't like yourself."

She remained quiet.

"Do you like yourself? When you look into a mirror what is it that you see? And does that please you?"

Camille thought about his question and figured she could probably end this conversation without ever answering him, but she decided not to take that route. "Each morning I wake up and take a shower. I look into the mirror and I see a woman who has had a hard childhood, who has lost a very important part of her life and who has built a wonderfully successful business. It's not until I step out of my apartment and into the real world that I see something else. No, I don't think I'm obese and I know that compared to others my plight is not so bad but there are some days when I'm just so uncomfortable. You have no idea what it's like to hear every day for years that you aren't good enough, you aren't pretty enough or dainty enough. It takes its toll."

"She did that to you." It was a statement from him, not a question.

Camille sighed. "I can't continue to blame her. My therapist told me that. I am who I am now because of me. And I'm generally not obsessive about my weight and my looks but when a guy like you… I mean, when a man shows interest in me when I know there are hundreds of other women he could be looking at, it's a bit unbelievable."

"Again, you underestimate yourself. I'm no saint, Camille. Not by a long shot. But, yes, I am interested in you, all of you. I like your smile because I've never seen one so genuinely pretty before. And I like your ambition because it matches my own. I really like your curves because you have no idea what it does to me to see you walk in or out of a room."

She laughed because he sounded so tortured by that statement. "You know what I like about you, Adam?"

"What's that?"

"I like that you get me. You seem to know what I'm feeling or what I'm going through before I've even figured it out. Nobody's ever done that before. Well, except for Dana but that's because she's nosy and she's like a sister to me."

"I wish I was still there with you," he said out of the blue.

Pulling her covers around her tightly Camille let his words sink in, then responded, "I wish you were, too."

MILLIONAIRE PLAYBOY SETS HIS SIGHTS ON LOCAL FASHION DIVA

That was the headline in Saturday's edition of the *Times*. Camille had just finished the article when her phone rang.

"Hello?"

"Have you seen it?" Dana asked immediately.

She sighed. "Yes."

"I wanted to be the first to call you and say that it's a bunch of bull. I think Adam really likes you. I watched him watching you last night and there didn't seem to be another person in that room for him besides you."

"It's okay, Dana. I'm fine with it. I know his reputation and I'm not getting my hopes up." But she was no longer thinking that she wasn't good enough for him. They stayed on the phone for an hour and a half last night, well earlier this morning, and when they hung up she was as convinced as Adam was that there was something special going on between them. She'd agreed not to overanalyze what that something special was right now but to just go with the flow.

"See, that's the thing, Camille. I think you *should* get your hopes up. Would a playboy summon a private jet to be here for your fashion show? Would he get up on that stage, and coerce his brother to get up on that stage, and model? I think he might be the one."

"Just because you found your knight in shining armor doesn't mean there's one out there for me. However, I'm willing to explore where this might lead."

"But there is, he's already rescued you once," Dana said and Camille could tell she was smiling.

"That's cute but I'm not as romantic as you are."

After hanging up with Dana, Camille reread the article.

The odd couple of the season, Camille Davis of CK Davis Designs, a fashion house that specializes in designs for the overweight, but has made millions in Tinsel Town from superstar clientele joins personal forces with Adam Donovan, real estate tycoon from Las Vegas. Donovan's previous relationships run the gamut from supermodels to politician's daughters. This is the first time his interests have appeared more rounded.

She didn't miss the slur but didn't want to think about it too deeply. Their telephone conversation last night proved that Adam Donovan was above the physical where women were concerned. Still, it was hard to read the thoughts that had traveled through her mind.

Tired of worrying over it Camille slipped into her spandex pants and T-shirt. Her extra bedroom had been converted into a gym because she didn't like being on display when she worked out. She switched on the radio and decided to start with free weights. Counting cleared her mind and focused her on the matter at hand. She'd never be a size two or six, but she would be healthy and in shape, whatever size she wore.

"So you're staying the whole weekend?" Linc asked. "Mom and Dad are due back tonight. You know she's going to want to have dinner tomorrow night."

"I should be back by then. I just don't want to leave her yet." Adam was dressed and talking to Linc on his cell phone as he left the hotel.

"Look, bro, I came to your defense yesterday when you stormed into my office demanding the jet. You said it was an emergency with this woman and I didn't question you. But you know Trent is about to have her and that wicked stepmother of hers investigated."

"Trent needs to find a woman to occupy his mind," Adam quipped.

Linc chuckled. "Like you did."

Adam didn't respond. Camille was not his woman. But she did mean something to him. "It's not that serious, Linc."

"I can't tell, Adam. You were a little defensive of her when she was here a few weeks ago and now this. Look, if you're feeling her, that's fine. Nobody's saying anything bad about her. Actually, Jade and I like her a lot. But I'd be remiss if I didn't say this—" Linc paused.

"Go ahead and say it. I wouldn't want you to be remiss," Adam said as he climbed into the rental car.

"She's different. I mean, she doesn't do battle well, you saw how she reacted when her stepmother arrived. Just take it easy with her."

Adam and Linc spoke for another few minutes about family issues and business deals. He was just outside of Camille's apartment when he paused to give Linc's words some serious thought.

Camille was different, but it was that difference that attracted him to her. That and her great breasts. The last thing he wanted to do was hurt her in any way but given his track record with women and his self-imposed distance rules, he wasn't sure that if he continued to pursue her he'd be able to prevent it.

For that reason alone he should walk away. But then he remembered the article in this morning's paper that had been so graciously included with his breakfast tray. Whatever progress he'd made in convincing her that her physical appearance had no bearing on how he felt about her may have been undone by that black-and-white print. For that reason alone, he had to see her.

He was at the door to her apartment building when his cell phone rang. "Adam Donovan."

"Hi, Adam. I was wondering if today was a good day for us to get together."

With two fingers Adam squeezed the bridge of his nose. "I thought we had this discussion already, Kim."

"You can't keep avoiding me. Sooner or later

we're going to meet up and we're going to settle this," she said.

"There's nothing to settle."

"We were going to spend the rest of our lives together."

"And you walked away from that," he yelled. Then he took a deep breath. "Look, this is pointless. There is nothing for us to talk about and should we happen to run into each other that fact will still hold true. Harassing me won't change that." He disconnected the line before she had a chance to come back with a response, although he knew that was only delaying the inevitable.

Taking the elevator up to Camille's apartment Adam tried like hell to clear his mind of thoughts of Kim. Why had she come back, now of all times? During those first few weeks he'd waited, desperately, hoping that she'd just gotten cold feet and would come back saying she still loved him, still wanted to marry him. But she hadn't. He'd made peace with that fact and he'd moved on, determined to never let another woman hurt him that way.

He knocked on Camille's door, careful to keep his growing confusion from turning into anger and causing his fist to go through the door. He was about to knock again when she pulled it open.

As if his mind weren't already reeling she had the nerve to answer the door in pants that fit her legs and thighs precisely and a T-shirt melded to her torso by sweat. For a minute he paused to consider if a sweaty woman was really sexy… Ah, yeah, definitely.

"Hey," she said, obviously out of breath. "What are you doing here?"

"I was lonely and wanted someone to show me around L.A.," he said, a smile tickling his lips.

She tilted her head as if she were deciding whether or not to believe him. Then she stepped to the side and let him in. "I'm sure this isn't your first time in L.A. I know this because you've been to my father's house. But I guess I'm game to being tour guide if you want."

She closed the door once he was inside and he turned to get another look at her. "Sorry for interrupting your exercise session." Her hair was pulled back into a ponytail, her forehead and neck still damp. An uncontrollable urge arose and he took a step closer, needing to kiss her, to place his lips at the base of her neck, to stop that line of sweat traveling beneath the rim of her shirt.

"It's okay. Saturday mornings are the only time I really have to myself. Just let me grab a shower and I'll be ready."

She attempted to walk past him but he touched her arm, pulling her back up against him. "You look really good," he whispered.

She laughed. "You've got to be kidding. I'm sweaty, wearing too-tight clothes and haven't combed my hair since I woke up."

He touched her cheek, let his finger glide over

the damp skin until he touched her lower lip. "Really good," he repeated.

"Are you okay?" she asked suddenly. "You're acting strange."

"I'm fine," he said, then leaned forward to kiss her quickly. "Go shower. I'll wait."

She disappeared into the other room and Adam let out a breath. What was he doing?

"I had a great time today," Camille said honestly when they returned to her apartment at nearly ten o'clock Saturday evening.

"So did I. I've never had such a pretty tour guide before." Again Adam removed the key from her door and closed it after he'd entered.

Her legs burned from all the walking they'd done but she wasn't tired. She was pleasantly exhausted. Adam had surprised her by showing up at her door earlier today. She'd planned to go to the office after her workout to get a handle on all the orders that came in from the show, but his idea of sightseeing around L.A. sounded so much better.

They'd found a cute little bistro and had lunch, then strolled the streets window shopping and getting to know each other. Surprisingly, they had a lot in common. Each of them were workaholics and they loved chocolate ice cream. Outside of that, Camille concluded that Adam was really down to earth. There wasn't an uppity, superior bone in his body. He liked people and had even struck up conversations with several strangers while they were in furniture stores.

And, yes, he was very charismatic with the ladies. The salesperson in the fabric store they visited had thrown herself at him from the moment they walked in the door. She hadn't given Camille more than a second glance until Adam announced that he and his wife were looking for fabric for drapes in their new home. The woman had quickly backed down and even sent another salesperson to help them. Although she was initially uncomfortable with Adam's lie she eventually found the woman's reaction funny instead of humiliating, and continued shopping.

Adam had that effect on her. Things that normally would have crushed her spirit didn't seem so bad with him by her side. Maybe because he didn't feed into any of it or maybe it was the way he held tight to her hand or brushed her hair back from her face. These actions made her feel special, cherished almost.

"Well, this tour guide has officially retired. And the next time I come to Vegas you owe me big-time." Slipping her shoes off Camille crossed her legs beneath her and turned to face him as she sat on the couch. He'd taken the seat next to her as she'd expected.

"Most definitely," he said with a smile. "There's a lot more to Vegas than the casinos I'd like to show you."

"I'd like to see that house again. You know the one we had lunch at. Are you finished building it?"

Adam had lain his head back on the couch so she had a great side profile of him. His strong chin was covered with a light coating of hair and she found herself wondering how he'd look with a full beard. He had thick eyebrows which gave him a sexy but dangerous look until you got a glance at his eyes. The eyes and that smile were deadly; Camille had already figured that out and tried to react to both appropriately.

"Not yet. I don't get as much time to focus on it as I'd like."

"So it is your house?" she asked.

He turned his head to look at her. "No. I mean, not exactly. My cousin Ben, Max's brother, will be moving back to the States in a couple of months and he asked us to get something together for him. I got the land in a package deal with another property we'd already sold so we figured we'd take this opportunity to build something from scratch."

"Where is your cousin living now?"

"He works for the FBI and for the last four years has been on assignment in Rome."

Camille was shocked. "We have jurisdiction in Rome?"

Adam smiled. "It's a long story." He took her hand in his. "One that I'd rather not spend my time with you talking about."

All thoughts of FBI and international jurisdiction fled Camille's mind. She loved when he touched her. Looking down at her hand in his she felt a sense of security coupled with longing. And reality threatened to intercede.

"Hey, what happened?" Adam asked with concern.

Camille blinked and focused on him again. "What do you mean?"

"Your facial expression changed, you looked seriously stressed for a minute. What were you thinking?"

"Nothing," she answered quickly.

Adam sighed. "You know, when I first came over my purpose was to reassure you."

"Reassure me about what?"

"I saw the article, Camille. And I'm fairly positive that you did, too."

He'd moved a little closer and still held her hand. She tried for a light tone. "What makes you think I read the paper?"

With his other hand he stroked her cheek. "Because you're a very smart woman and you'd want to know what was said about your showing last night."

She hunched her shoulders, not really wanting to discuss the hurtful words that had been printed. "It's no big deal."

"That's what I said, but then again, I'm used to being lied about and misconstrued."

"Really?"

He nodded. "Yeah, it's tough being one of the Triple Threat Brothers."

"I'm afraid to ask," Camille said, chuckling.

"It's a silly nickname my brothers and I earned by Vegas's socially elite. A few years back it was said that we were a triple threat to all women because we were each good looking, had money and were basically unattainable."

She shifted and acted as if she were examining his face carefully. "Okay, I see the good-looking part and without a look at your bank statements I'm pretty sure by the private jet your family owns that you do have money, but you've got me stumped on unattainable."

He tweaked her nose. "Very funny."

"I'm serious. I mean, unless you're not into women, why would you be unattainable?" She knew why it wasn't possible for her to have him, but there were plenty of women who could possibly steal Adam's heart.

"Because that's the way we like it. Long-term relationships weren't on any of our lists of achievements. And after a few women we've dated got that impression they started talking. Rumors boost circulation."

"But Linc married Jade," Camille said slowly. The room was dark and she was alone, sitting closely on the couch with Adam. They'd had a really good day together and she'd almost thought it was the perfect date. But what he'd just said raised more alarm in her mind.

"That was amazing. He and Jade had an affair

in college and then she turned up in his life again. At first he didn't want to think about anything permanent, but I guess she changed his mind."

She'd begun twirling the gold necklace she wore around her finger, her mind totally focused on the fact that Adam was basically admitting to not wanting a relationship. "They seem to be very much in love."

Adam recognized the shift in her mood from the sound of her voice and wanted to kick himself. He'd readily admitted that his intention today was to assure her that his interest in her was genuine. And yet he'd told her about his reputation. There was no doubt in his mind what she was thinking now. He immediately released her hand, shifted so that they were face-to-face and cupped her cheeks. "Linc loves his wife very much, proving that the Triple Threat Brothers story is all rumor and speculation. They don't know us or what we want in our hearts, in our lives."

She looked at him seriously and Adam felt himself falling into the deep brown pools of her eyes. His thumb grazed her bottom lip and he moved in closer. "They don't know what I want."

She licked her lips and Adam felt his groin tighten. "What do you want, Adam?"

Damn! He was positive she had no idea what she was really asking him. If she did she wouldn't be so calmly waiting for his reply. He couldn't possibly tell her that he wanted her naked, hot body beneath him, poised and ready for his possession.

And he didn't dare tell her that the urge to feel her nipples against his tongue, her wetness on his lips, was threatening to drive him insane.

But he wasn't in any mood to lie to her, either.

"I want to kiss you."

She surprised him with a small smile as she leaned in closer. "Then do it."

That was all the prompting Adam needed. He'd intended to take her lips slowly, to slip his tongue into her mouth and languidly stroke her until she moaned for more. But his blood was pumping so loud and fierce through his veins that his mind was a bit distorted. So the second he was close enough his lips plundered hers, pulling the soft flesh of her bottom lip between his teeth. He sucked until she hissed and then he swiped his tongue over the now swollen lip, her bottom row of teeth. Her hands went to his chest and she kneaded urgently.

Adam's entire body shook with desire and he thrust his tongue into her mouth. He'd expected her to let him retain the lead, guiding them both into a blissfully romantic kiss. But she captured his tongue instead, sucking it greedily into her mouth and holding on. He groaned and raked his fingers through her hair.

They devoured each other hungrily, groping and tugging at clothing until her blouse was unbuttoned and his shirt was pulled completely from the band of his pants.

The moment his hand cupped her breast she

hissed. He whispered her name and wanted nothing more than to take the plump mound into his mouth but then he paused. Pulling both his mouth and hand away from her he moved back across the couch so that there was at least a foot of space between them.

He'd glanced at her briefly as he moved away, saw the complete look of confusion on her face and cursed himself silently.

Rubbing his hands down his face he took a deep, steadying breath. What the hell was he doing? This was Camille, his business partner and, as of lately, his friend. Yes, he wanted badly to make love to her and at this moment he figured she wanted the same thing. But he couldn't. Something just wasn't right.

He heard her whisper his name and struggled for something to say to her. Looking over at her in that instant he knew she didn't understand. Hell, he didn't quite understand it himself. The kiss had been great, intoxicating actually. She'd been soft and pliant in his arms. He was hard as steel in his pants. There was nothing stopping them from reaching for the pleasure they both knew would come from their joining. Nothing but him.

"Camille," he began.

"No." She quickly began shaking her head. "Don't say anything." Her fingers trembled as she buttoned her shirt.

She wouldn't look at him now and he knew that she was embarrassed, knew that she'd been thinking the absolute worst of the situation. She stood and tried to walk away when he stood up and blocked her retreat.

"Camille," he whispered, grabbing her by the shoulders. "Listen to me."

"You don't have to explain. It's okay. I'm okay," she said, looking across the room.

"It's not okay," he said and grasped her chin, turning her to face him. "Believe me when I say that I want you more than I've ever wanted any other woman in my life."

She opened her mouth to speak and he touched her lips with his fingertips. "I don't want you thinking for one moment that what just happened was a result of anything you'd done wrong. It's me."

"No. Don't lie on my account," she said softly. "You're perfect."

Adam threw back his head and laughed. "Not hardly." He gazed into her eyes and knew now why he couldn't take her to bed tonight. "You are the closest thing to a perfect woman that I've been privileged to come by. You are blatantly honest, frighteningly intelligent and sexier than you can possibly imagine."

"Then why did you stop?"

Her tongue skittered over her bottom lip and he lowered his forehead to hers and groaned. "What are you doing to me?" he murmured.

She shrugged. "Do you want to keep things on

a business only level? If we obviously want different things, maybe that's for the best."

He was already shaking his head negatively. "No." He took a deep breath and repeated, "No. There's no way I can continue to work with you and not want to touch you. And if I can't touch you or call you when I just want to hear your voice I'll go crazy."

She reached up a hand and rubbed his cheek. "Then, Adam, I really don't understand."

"I'm not real sure what's going on myself. All I know is that I enjoy being with you. A lot. Tomorrow morning I'm going to hate getting on that plane and heading back to Vegas because I know you'll still be here." He leaned into her touch, loving the feel of her hands on him and closed his eyes a moment to gather his thoughts. "I don't want to make any mistakes with you, Camille." And that was the truth. She was fragile, her emotions an open forum for anyone to take advantage of. Above all else he wanted to protect her from all hurt and harm. Even if that meant protecting her from himself.

"I'm a grown woman, Adam. I can handle an affair with you."

And those words were his undoing. He knew the moment she'd said them that he was going to say something that he hadn't given any thought to, that he hadn't considered in a very long time. "I don't want an affair with you, Camille. When I look at you I see so much more than a couple months of really good sex."

She giggled. "How do you know it'll be really good?"

He gave her a smirk then brushed a finger over her breast. "Trust me, I know."

Her body tensed against his and he let out a whoosh of air. "Yes, I definitely know. But I want more than that for us. Do you understand what I'm trying to say?"

Camille understood his words but couldn't believe the underlying truth in them. And she couldn't think straight over the loud thumping of her heart. This could not be happening to her. Good things like this did *not* happen to her.

This was the man who wanted to buy her father's house and sell it to some strangers. He was a reputed playboy, a savvy businessman, a loyal brother and a threat to her libido. And he was saying that he wanted a real relationship with her. Camille wanted to scream like she knew Dana would when she told her.

"I understand," she said in as calm a voice as she could muster.

"So you understand but what do you think about that?" he asked, still holding her in his arms.

He was staring at her intently, his hands moving freely up and down her side, where she knew he could feel her slight bulge and for a minute she almost reverted back to her insecurities about her body. She took a deep breath, determined to have faith in his words about liking her the way she was. "I think that we're both mature enough to know what we want. If you say you want something more, then I believe you."

He nodded, his hands resting at her sides, and she shifted trying to get them to move farther up and around her back.

"What do you want, Camille?"

She wanted him to throw her on that floor and make wild, passionate love to her. She wanted him to fall desperately in love with her the way she was afraid she was doing with him. She wanted the type of love Linc and Jade seemed to share. She wanted the happiness she'd seen on Jade's face. And then she knew she wanted the impossible.

So as she'd learned to do all her life, she decided to take whatever she could get. "I want to be with you in whatever capacity that I can."

Adam opened his mouth to say something and Camille knew she didn't want to hear it. What she wanted was his lips on hers and since he wasn't making that move she did it for him, effectively ending the conversation.

Chapter 8

Beverly Donovan sat to her husband's left at the head of the table in the dining room of their Las Vegas home. They'd just returned from an eight-week international cruise. She loved the time alone with her husband but admitted to being homesick after the first few days. A good portion of her life revolved around her family, her kids especially, and even though they were all grown up, she felt she was needed at home to make sure things were running smoothly. Still, whenever Henry said it was time for them to take a trip, to spend some time alone, she happily packed her bags. He was her husband and she loved him.

However, from her viewpoint this time she'd stayed away too long. Linc and Jade had come over for dinner as they usually did when there was a family meal planned. And Jade's younger sister, Noelle joined them, as well. Beverly's gaze rested on the energetic young woman for a minute. She was pretty as a picture but still had a lot of growing to do. She'd calmed down substantially in the months that Jade and Linc had been married, so much so that the job Linc had offered her in the casino almost a year ago had promoted her to shift manager where she seemed to be thoroughly enjoying herself.

Her nephew Max also decided to join them. He was the spitting image of his father, Henry's brother, Everette. Everette's boys had always spent a lot of time at her house and she loved them as if they were her own sons. As such she had high expectations for their lives, as well. Truth be told Beverly wanted to see all her nieces and nephews happy in marriage with kids and successful in business. That was an ambitious goal she knew, but it wasn't impossible.

Trent sat across from her brooding about something or other, but then that was Trent's way. He'd always been her most serious child to the point that he seemed agitated most of the time. Tonight his brow was drawn so tight she could probably bounce quarters off of it. He looked to be in deep thought. After dinner she'd have to find out about what.

And then there was her baby boy, Adam. He was such a handsome man now that he'd turned thirty. His boyish cuteness had grown into an allure that she'd watched women battle for. Unlike her older two sons Adam always had a twinkle in his eyes and a joke on his lips. He was carefree but great with business. The company he and Max ran together was doing a wonderful job and she couldn't be more proud of him. Tonight, however, Adam resembled Trent a little too closely.

While all her sons had her husband's deep brown eyes and strong build they were each different in their own way. Adam had the smooth almond complexion and wore his dark wavy hair cropped close to his head. He had allowed a goatee to grow in and it was cut precisely giving him an older, distinguished look. But that wasn't the only difference Beverly noticed in her son tonight. He was abnormally quiet.

"So, Adam, Max was telling me this morning that you've entered a different type of business venture. Something about a house in Los Angeles," she said hoping he would extend the conversation to the woman who currently owned the property. The woman who Max had also mentioned captured Adam's attention.

Adam was sipping his wine so he took a moment before answering. "It's a great property that I had the chance to see inside and out before the previous owner passed away. We made an offer to the new owner but then ran into a—" he paused a moment, gazing across the room out the window. "A guess you could say a roadblock. Only she moved out of our way in her own time."

Beverly raised a brow and noticed the smile on Jade's face as Adam had spoken. "Oh, the owner's a woman?" she questioned.

"Yes, ma'am. As a matter of fact she's Camille Davis of CK Davis Designs."

There it was, that light she was so used to seeing in Adam's eyes. Funny how it brightened at the mention of this woman. "Really? I was just reading a magazine article about her on the plane ride home. She's a pretty young thing. And she built that business all by herself. Talented and pretty, that's a good combination."

Jade seemed anxious to add her opinion to this conversation. "She's also very nice, Ms. Beverly. We went to her show on Friday and she was a very gracious host. You have to see the new dresses I bought when we were there."

"I read about the show. She received rave reviews. I've been saying that I needed to pick up some more of her pieces." Beverly kept her eye on Adam as she spoke.

"Oh, I have her newest catalog and she told me to just give her a call when I needed something. We can go to lunch tomorrow and look through it," Jade offered.

"Can I look at it?" Noelle asked. "The casino's

having a big party for New Year's Eve and I wanted something really nice to wear."

"Nicer than all the other dresses and outfits you've purchased in the last few months?" Jade asked jokingly. "I don't know what the general manager was thinking giving you a raise. In a minute you're going to need a new house with a room full of closets for all your clothes and shoes."

Noelle chuckled. "A girl's got to have some indulgence in her life. Mine is clothes and shoes." Then she stared at the ceiling thoughtfully. "And chocolate and mystery novels."

Linc laughed. "Your whole life is an indulgence, Noelle. That's one of the things I like about you. You live life to its fullest every day."

Noelle shrugged, lifting her glass to her lips. "Life's too short to waste time. I don't know how long I have here so I intend to make every day count. Right, Adam?"

Adam had only been half listening to the conversation. His mind and, if he were not mistaken, a small portion of his heart, were still in L.A. "That's right. No sense in wasting time."

He glanced at Noelle and couldn't help smiling along with her. Almost the mirror image of Jade, Noelle had a sharp wit and an infectious laugh. After the wedding he'd quickly grown attached to her, loving the idea of having a younger sister to look out for. Although Noelle wasn't too keen on the protectiveness of the Donovan men when it came to their women and as such she'd had her share of arguments with Linc, Trent and even Adam about her choice of men. She'd fit into this family as smoothly as Jade had and Adam couldn't help but wonder if the woman he chose would have such an easy transition.

Wait a minute, since when was he thinking of choosing a woman? Ever since the Kim debacle he'd been sworn to bachelorhood. And while Linc had been the first to school him on the art of being single, his older brother had blissfully fallen in love and settled down. Adam wondered if it would end that way for him.

"So Ms. Davis changed your course of business, huh, son?" Henry entered the conversation.

"I guess you could say that. She really has a good head for business. The deal she struck was different but had advantages that Donovan Investments couldn't ignore," Adam said.

Max nodded his agreement. "I was a bit skeptical at first but she made a good argument. Besides, we had to take into consideration that it was her family home and her father hasn't been gone for that long. I think she's still grieving," he said, then looked to Adam.

"She is taking his loss really hard. Her mother passed away when she was young and that stepmother of hers is a trip."

Beverly watched Adam carefully. "That's such a shame for a girl to have lost her mother. Jade, you and Noelle should spend some time with her. You've been through the grieving process, maybe you can offer her some support."

"You're probably right. She doesn't have any siblings so I can imagine this is a very hard time for her. Although her business partner, Dana, seems really close to her, it might be nice if she could talk to someone who's been through a similar experience." Jade continued to nod her agreement. "I think I'll call her tomorrow to see when she's free. Maybe I'll invite her to the house for a girls' weekend."

"That sounds nice," Beverly said. "What do you think, Adam? Do you think Camille would like to come for a visit?"

"I'm sure she'd be very thankful for the distraction." Only he would be the one distracted and much more than he was now.

He'd left her house last night after indulging in a couple more steamy kisses that proved to be a test in his resolve. But he'd meant what he said to her. He and Camille were on uncharted territory, meaning it had been a very long time since he'd thought about a woman along the lines that he found himself thinking of her. She'd seemed to accept that explanation but Adam wasn't entirely certain that she believed him. That's why it was more important than ever for him to refrain from sleeping with her. She was ready for an affair, prepared for him to take her then leave her.

And he, surprisingly, was not. In fact, the thought of leaving her this morning had been so difficult for a solid hour he'd entertained excuses he could make for staying in L.A. In the end he knew that the space would do them both some good. He had to get a grip on this new direction their relationship was taking and he suspected Camille needed time to acclimate herself to the things he'd said.

But make no mistake about it, their separation would not be for long. He fully intended to keep seeing Camille and where that was leading, he was eagerly going to find out.

The family had adjourned to the den after dessert, Jade and Noelle sitting by the fire most likely discussing Jade's spa or Noelle's fantastic stories of working in the casino while Trent, Max, Linc and Henry enjoyed cigars and talk of stocks and trading. Adam had found a seat near the window and peered outside to the dark evening sky.

He was deep in thought and so didn't hear his mother's approach until she'd taken a seat in the chair next to him.

"The sky seems so still tonight. No stars, no clouds, just a peaceful darkness," she said absently. "Nights like this are good for cuddling with someone you love."

Adam grinned. The love his parents shared was obvious and enviable. "Are you saying that you and Dad are about to turn in for the night?"

Beverly chuckled. "Oh, no, not just yet. We've had a lot of alone time. A lot of peaceful nights to do what we do."

Adam didn't even want to think of what they do. "Okay, you're bordering on releasing too much information, Mom."

She waved a hand. "You are no stranger to the goings-ons between men and women."

He nodded. "You've got a point. But my parents are off-limits when it comes to the activities of men and women."

"How do you think you got here?" Beverly asked with another hearty chuckle.

Adam covered his ears. "Mom, please," he moaned.

"All right. All right. I'll stop teasing you." But she did reach out and take her son's hand in hers. "Something's different about you tonight, son. You want to tell me what's going on?"

"No," Adam said quickly.

Beverly released his hand. "Well, that won't stop me from asking. What's bothering you?"

"Nothing. I'm just a little drained from working and then the trip this weekend."

"Yes, the trip to L.A., to the CK Designs fall show. To my knowledge you've never been to a fashion show before, have you?"

Adam sensed where this conversation was going. "I'm very into today's fashions. I like to look good when I'm buying and selling property."

"That you do," Beverly nodded. "But I get the distinct impression there was more to this trip than just the latest designs."

"It was. Camille was very nervous about the showing. I wanted to offer her some support."

"So she means something to you, something other than business."

"Her peace of mind will help the business deal," he said and felt regret at the words. He didn't make a habit of lying to his mother.

"I'm sure she was very appreciative. I really think it would be nice for Jade and Noelle to offer her some support, as well."

"That is a good idea. I hope she takes them up on it."

"And what else do you hope where Camille Davis is concerned, Adam?"

He wouldn't look at her. His mother was the smartest woman he knew. The fact that she'd come over and brought up the subject of Camille attested to that. "To be honest, I don't really know."

"But you're trying to figure it out?"

"Yes, ma'am."

Beverly reached for her son's hand again. "Then let me give you some advice, be open to any and everything when it comes to a woman you are genuinely interested in. And don't live in the past."

Camille was in her office on Thursday afternoon. Her week had been tremendously busy with special orders from high-end clients, as well as numerous requests for interviews. Talk shows, tabloid magazines, you name it, they had contacted her office for an exclusive. She'd taken the chance on showing all three lines together, one that many designers before her had shied away from. She was proud of the fact that it had turned out to be a whopping success. Still she'd be lying if she didn't say she was impressed by the attention Adam's appearance at her show had garnered her company.

But then she came back down to earth and realized the real reason behind them contacting her. They were nosy, lying bloodhounds out for the next story to sell their product. She couldn't blame them too much since profit was her bottom line, too, only she didn't sacrifice anybody's reputation or livelihood to get ahead. On the first run she'd turned all interview and appearance requests not directly related to CK Designs down flat. All calls after that she ignored.

Thankfully she was entirely too busy to even consider what they would write without her consent. Already she'd seen another article about Adam and Trent modeling for the show. That one was entertaining until it hinted at her giving the Donovan men special favors to boost her sales. So now, not only was she the "round" but successful fashion diva dating above herself, but she was apparently offering her body as compensation. Where did they come up with this stuff?

Sometime on Tuesday evening she decided that she would focus on work only. If it didn't have to do with her designs or orders coming in she didn't want to hear about it. Except when Adam called—and he did so regularly. She had to smile at that thought. He called her in the morning before she left her apartment to say good morning and he called her in the evening after nine, when they were both supposedly no longer on the clock, to say good night.

Normally she didn't talk to him during the day but he'd called her at the office yesterday with news about the house. The renovations should be done before Thanksgiving and he wanted her to go with him to inspect them. She'd readily agreed. She hadn't been back to the house since she'd packed and she was anxious to see how it looked now. Her heart still hurt at the thought of never stepping foot in her family home again but lately she'd been more excited about the finished product than sad about the loss it would entail. She knew she owed the change of heart to one person in particular.

"I don't even have to ask what you're thinking about over there. Or should I say who you're thinking about. That goofy smile says it all," Dana said as she propped her legs up on the end of Camille's desk and relaxed in her chair.

Camille turned to face her, trying like hell to stop smiling, but only making the smile more noticeable. "I won't deny it. I was thinking about him."

"That's a good thing."

She shrugged. "I guess so. But we need to be talking business. Did the shipments go out yesterday?"

Dana flipped through a folder she held on her lap. "They sure did. And the one to Jade Donovan arrived yesterday afternoon. I have the confirmation right here." She waved a pink slip of paper in the air.

"Great."

"I'd say. Mrs. Donovan dropped a whopping fifteen thousand on your latest. You may become her private designer before this is all over."

"I doubt it. But I'm glad she liked the clothes enough to buy something."

Dana frowned. "Buy something? Camille, are you delirious? She bought fifteen thousand dollars' worth of something in one evening! I'd say she liked a whole lot. And don't forget they were talking about putting your things in their casino. That is so huge."

"That was just a smokescreen for Moreen's benefit," Camille commented.

"You like to live your life with blinders on, don't you," Dana replied.

Camille stared at her in confusion. "What are you talking about? They came to the fashion show because Adam came and he only came because he thought I was having a nervous breakdown. Which, coincidentally, I probably was. They are a very supportive family."

Dana arched a brow. "Really? I thought Adam came because he wanted to be with you on one of the biggest nights of your life and his family came to also show their support. But I could be wrong."

Camille was about to comment when there was a knock on her door and then Sofari entered with a newspaper in hand. "I know you said you didn't want to read any more articles but I just had to show you this one."

She dropped the paper onto Camille's desk and Dana pulled her legs down and came around to read the article over Camille's shoulder.

Adam Donovan and Natalie Janica, daughter of Congressman Ople Janica, at the Breast Cancer Awareness Foundation Charity Ball last year.

This was the snippet beneath a picture that covered most of the page. Adam wore another tuxedo, the woman wrapped around him wore an emerald-green dress that hugged every curve she had and most likely created a couple more. She was beautiful with her dark, slanted eyes and high cheekbones. Her plump lips and impeccable makeup caused Camille's stomach to plummet.

Adam Donovan, the youngest of the Triple Threat Donovans is no stranger to women but now some would say he's set his sights a little lower. Camille Davis is not entirely out of

the Donovan circle, being the only child of
the famous Hollywood producer, Randolph
Davis, but socialites in Las Vegas are fuming
at how low Adam has apparently stooped.
Sources close to Donovan report their connection as solely a business deal, some real
estate and some dealing with CK Davis
Designs. But the couple was seen around Los
Angeles several times last weekend and
appeared to be doing a little more than
business.

This was followed up by two smaller photos.
One of Camille and her father taken at the premier
of his last movie almost two years and twenty
pounds ago, and the other was of her and Adam as
they had lunch at the bistro on Saturday afternoon.
She hadn't even realized they were being followed
or that they were being photographed. Dropping the
paper on the desk she sat back in her chair, her
good mood effectively deflated.

"Since when do you subscribe to Las Vegas
newspapers?" Dana asked when she'd lifted the
paper to have a closer look.

Camille let out a shaky breath. "I don't."

"Then how did this get here?" Dana looked to
Sofari for that answer.

"It was delivered this morning with all the other
papers. I thought Camille should see this one since
it had pictures of her and her father."

"I don't want to see any more articles. I don't care who they reference or what pictures they have," Camille said with finality.

Dana made a motion with her hands telling Sofari to leave the office. Then she placed a hand on Camille's shoulder. "It doesn't mean anything, Camille. You know how tabloids lie."

Camille nodded, attempting to stay optimistic, although the chips were steadily stacking against her. "I know that the words in print are usually lies. Pictures, on the other hand…"

"So what he's pictured with the congressman's daughter. He's not the first," Dana said flippantly. "Besides, this was last year. You can't hold his past against him."

"No," Camille said as she stood and faced the window, "I can't hold it against him. But I can take it into account." She rested her head on the window and closed her eyes. "What was I thinking?"

Dana grabbed her by the shoulders and turned her around. "You were thinking that here's a guy that's interested in you and you acted accordingly. None of this—" she motioned toward the newspaper "—discredits that fact. Adam Donovan likes you. I know it and the press knows it. That's obviously why they're making such a big deal out of it."

"But I don't want to be made a big deal out of. I don't want to be in the spotlight that way."

"I know that because of the private schools you were in and the social circles you chose to be a part of you managed to dodge a lot of the attention your father received, but honestly, Camille, let's face the facts. You're rich. You're successful. You design clothes that right now Hollywood stars are rushing to buy. Bottom line, you're going to be in the spotlight any way they can get you there."

Camille knew what Dana said was true, just as she knew she had no right to blame Adam for what was printed about him. He'd been nothing but honest with her about his reputation and the consequences of it. In fact, he'd seemed to hate it as much as she did. Still, he accepted it as one would accept a rainy day. He just opened an umbrella and kept on moving.

And regardless of her issues, she conceded that it was probably time she handled things the same way. She knew she wouldn't change the world's perception of her—she just had to be sure not to allow herself to get sucked into their misconceptions.

She didn't think she could handle it as easily.

"Camille, Jade Donovan is on the line for you," Sofari announced over the intercom.

Camille covered her face with her hands and took three steadying breaths. Her heart had picked up pace since reading the newspaper, but she was determined not to have a meltdown. Now she had this phone call to take. The last thing she needed was to crumble on the phone with Jade Donovan.

"She's probably calling to say thank you for the quick delivery," Dana offered.

Camille nodded, then slowly sat in her chair. Another deep breath and she was able to pick up the phone. "Hi, Jade. What can I do for you?"

"Hello, Camille. I'm actually calling for two reasons. One to thank you for the expeditious delivery of my items. I am so pleased and everything fit perfectly. I also told my mother-in-law about meeting you and just like I said she was sorry that she'd missed the opportunity."

"I'm glad you're pleased. You can tell your mother-in-law that I'll send her a first look of all the new lines if she'd like," Camille said, pleased at Jade's words.

"Actually, that's the second reason I was calling. You see, my sister would like to meet you as well, so I was thinking of a weekend meeting. Just us girls, like an endless slumber party for grown-ups." Jade laughed.

Camille found herself smiling, although she couldn't believe they were actually inviting her to come. "I don't know, Jade. I'm pretty busy."

"Girl, I can imagine. That new line is hot. I was especially impressed with the young-adult designs. It's about time somebody paid attention to the younger market in a positive way. That was a pretty bold move on your part and I commend you for going out on a limb. But I'm talking about the weekend. I'll have the jet pick you up Friday after work and then it'll bring you back home Sunday evening. You won't miss a minute of business time. But you've got to have some time just for you."

She remembered Adam's words and couldn't help but agree. Jade's kudos about her show also went a long way to boosting her self-esteem. While that article was hurtful, there was still a bright side. Her business was booming and Adam Donovan did seem extremely interested in her. She decided to go with the flow. "You're right."

"Of course I'm right. Now, I'll have my assistant fax you all the important info about pickups and drop-offs and I'll see you Friday night."

"Okay," Camille said with enthusiasm. "I'll see you Friday night."

"I don't know what she wants, Trent. That's why I came to you." Adam draped the towel he'd been using around his neck and sat on the bench in the locker room. He'd called Trent last night after he'd received another phone call from Kim. She was adamant about meeting up with him and he still couldn't figure out why. It must be something really important for her to continue calling him. But before he agreed to meet with her he wanted to know where she'd been for the last nine years.

Trent called him back this morning and suggested they meet at the gym. Adam hadn't been to the gym in about a week, he was so tied up with approving things for the Davis house and finishing

Ben's house since his cousin now indicated that he'd be back in the States before Christmas.

While they worked out he'd given Trent the rundown on Kim's calls. As he'd expected, and as he felt himself, Trent was suspicious.

"She's been gone for how long? Nine years? That's time enough to get in a lot of trouble." Trent sat on the bench beside Adam. "Or she could have been in trouble before she left."

"What kind of trouble?"

"I don't know. She was your girl, not mine. I'm just saying the way she's calling you sounds desperate. Now I remember Kim being a very attractive young woman, which means that she's probably a knockout now. You're my brother and I love you, but I don't see that she's in need of a man and wants you."

Adam bowed to him. "Thanks a lot, man."

Trent chuckled. "I'm serious. Besides, you've got your hands full with another woman. You don't have time for Kim Alvarez. But I agree her timing is suspicious as well as her tenacity. I'll look into it tomorrow."

"Thanks," Adam sighed.

"Now you wanna talk about what's really bothering you?"

Standing, Adam retrieved his shirt from his locker and slipped it over his head. "Nothing's bothering me."

"Denial is a waste of time with me and you know

there's nothing I hate more than wasting time. So cut the crap and tell me what's going on."

Trent was a no-nonsense man. He was a question-and-answer man. A bottom-line man. Adam respected that about him. His brother never seemed indecisive or confused about what he should or should not do. Adam envied that about him.

"I like Camille Davis," Adam said simply.

Trent slammed his locker closed and chuckled. "Is that all? Is that what has you all jacked up? Mom's worried sick about you. Max is afraid you're going to lose your business edge. And it's all about you liking Camille Davis."

"No. It's not just about me liking her. It's about me *really* liking her."

Trent paused between pulling on his pants and staring at his younger brother. "You act like this is a problem. Is it a problem?"

Adam exhaled a breath. "It's a problem for her because she doesn't believe me. And it's a problem for me because I know the consequences."

"And Kim's calling you out of the blue brings those consequences to the forefront? I see your dilemma. But I'm not the one for this conversation. You know my stance on women. Do what you need to do, for as long as you need to do it with them and move on. Don't give them anything of yourself besides the physical."

"I know. I know. You've told me all this before."

Adam had gone over all of this in his mind. He knew what his stance on women should be after what Kim did to him. He also knew what he felt for Camille, regardless of his past.

"Then what's the problem?" Trent put on his shirt and looked down at his brother.

"The problem is I can't give her the physical part of me without sacrificing myself."

"Wait a minute, are you saying you can't sleep with her?" Trent asked with confusion clearly written on his face.

"I'm saying I won't sleep with her just for the hell of it."

Trent made a low whistle. "First Linc and now you. Did I teach the two of you nothing?"

Adam couldn't help but laugh. "You taught us a lot, we just had the good sense not to follow your instructions."

"Then you shall suffer the same fate as Linc."

Adam lifted his gym bag on his shoulder. "Have you been around Linc and Jade lately? I don't think you could say he's suffering."

Trent smiled and fell into step beside Adam. "I have to agree with you there. He does seem really happy. Jade's good for him."

They walked out of the gym and were headed for their cars when Trent paused, clapping a hand on Adam's back. "I think Camille Davis might just be good for you, too."

Chapter 9

"**I**'m so glad you could make it," Jade said as she embraced Camille.

Camille had no choice but to hug her back even though she was unsure why this woman who barely knew her was being nice to her.

Just as Jade's itinerary had said, Camille was picked up at her apartment at seven that evening. She boarded the Donovan private jet at seven forty-five and at nine o'clock she was sitting in the back of a limo heading toward the home of Jade and Lincoln Donovan.

And what a home that was. It was huge and impeccably decorated from the two rooms she'd seen so far. Jade obviously had great taste in everything, including clothes.

"Thanks for inviting me."

"Don't mention it." Jade smiled as she took Camille's purse from her shoulder. "Now, come on into the kitchen. We're cooking a late dinner and then we're going to have brownies and the best damned homemade pound cake you've ever tasted for dessert."

Camille followed her but groaned in the process. Sweets were her weakness but memories of the struggle she went through to lose weight strengthened her resolve. "I can't have brownies and pound cake. Do you have any frozen yogurt?"

Jade paused just as they walked into the kitchen. "No way. This is a weekend of indulgence. And I am not going to watch you eat frozen yogurt while I pig out. I didn't invite you to my house to torture me."

For a minute Camille didn't know what to say; then Jade smiled and she released the breath she'd been holding.

"You'll eat cake and brownies just like us."

"You can put frozen yogurt on top of your cake, though." A female that Camille didn't know spoke. One look at her and she knew this had to be Jade's sister. They had the same slanted eyes. Jade's coloring was more exotic than her sister and she was an inch or so taller, but they still had a strong resemblance.

"Thanks. I'm Camille Davis." Camille extended her hand to the woman.

Noelle waved her hand away and gave Camille a hug. "It's good to finally meet you. I'm Noelle, Jade's sister."

What was it with these people and hugging? Camille thought. Coming from a household where Moreen was in charge didn't exactly prepare her for an abundance of female kindness. But Camille had resigned herself to be open this weekend. She'd been invited here for a fun-filled weekend and she was determined to make the most of it.

"So what are we having for dinner?" she asked happily.

He was not going to go see her.

This weekend was for the girls. Jade had made a point of explaining that to him again last night when he'd shown up at her spa.

Adam drummed his fingers on his desk blotter. He'd known the moment the Donovan jet landed because he'd phoned the pilot earlier in the day and requested that he notify him when he returned from Los Angeles.

That was more than two hours ago. It was now almost midnight and he was still at his office. He'd been working like a madman all week long. Quite the contrary to what he'd told Camille about enjoying life. But the second he entered his apartment he'd found himself bombarded with thoughts of her. He called her every day desperate to hear her voice and they'd been talking amicably. Actually, they'd been talking like two teenagers in high school way into the wee hours of the morning about anything and nothing.

So he really liked her, that wasn't so bad. And so he was really horny thinking of her in bed in one of Jade's guest rooms. With a curse he stood from his chair and paced his office. He had two choices: call her or go home and take a cold shower.

He did neither.

A half hour later he was pulling up in front of Linc's house. Turning off the ignition he sat in the car staring at the house. Which room would she be in? He knew the layout to Linc's house like the back of his hand since this had been one of his renovation projects. There were three levels; the basement housed Linc's gym and Jade's massive library. The main level held the living room, dining room, den, kitchen and sunroom. The second level had four bedrooms and a master suite along with four bathrooms and two home offices, one for Jade and one for Linc.

The windows for the master suite were all facing the back of the house. Linc wanted to wake up to the sun rising over the mountaintops. Adam scanned the windows of the second level debating which one it would be. He'd been concentrating so hard that he hadn't heard anyone approach. So when the tapping on his window sounded he nearly jumped into the passenger seat.

Looking out the window he glimpsed Linc standing with one hand in his pocket, a goofy grin on his face. Pressing the button he watched the window slide down.

"You know if you weren't related I'd be kicking your ass right about now?" Linc said casually.

"But I am related so I'd appreciate you not scaring ten years off my life." Adam put the window back up and opened the car door to get out. Pressing the alarm, he stood in front of the car looking back up at the house.

"I'm pretty sure Jade won't appreciate company at this hour." Linc was still grinning.

Clearly Adam hadn't thought this through. This was his brother's house but it was almost one o'clock in the morning. A friendly visit this most definitely was not. To hell with it, he wasn't about to lie to Linc. Most likely because he was sure Linc already knew why he was here.

"I just thought I'd drop by to say hi," he said in a voice he hoped was casual.

Linc nodded. "You couldn't wait until morning? Or better yet, you couldn't have come over earlier this evening?"

"Jade warned me not to interrupt them last night. You heard her, she wasn't joking."

"Yes, I heard her. Which has me asking again why you would come over here at this time of night? If Jade warned you about coming over earlier—"

"All right!" Adam yelled, then thought of what time it was and lowered his voice. "I came to see Camille because I tried not to come earlier this evening but lost that battle and ended up here anyway. And I know it sounds ridiculous and totally out of character for me but it is what it is. Now, I'd like for you to tell me which room she's in." He paused then looked at his brother fully dressed with a jacket on. "What are you doing coming in at this hour?"

Linc chuckled. "Lucky for you Jade also ordered me out of the house tonight. So I stayed at the casino for as long as I could without falling asleep on the craps table." He walked away, heading up the front steps. "Come on if you're coming."

Adam followed knowing that he was going to catch hell tomorrow morning when Linc had a chance to tell Trent and Max what he'd done. Strangely enough he didn't care. As long as he got to see Camille.

They were greeted with laughter the moment they entered the house. Continuing to follow Linc through the foyer and past the living room they entered the den, which was covered in darkness except for the candles lit around the room.

"Good evening, or good morning, ladies," Linc said with a slow smile.

Three incredibly beautiful women looked up

from their position on the floor and all but one of them smiled in greeting.

Camille's gaze found Adam's instantly and held. He wasn't sure if she was shocked or angry by the sight of him. But at this point didn't really care. He walked in past Linc. "Hello," he said, moving closer to where Camille sat.

Jade jumped up, putting a hand on his chest. "What are you doing here? I thought I told you to stay away," she said with mock anger.

"I know. You did. But—" Adam paused. "How come you're not yelling at him?" he asked, pointing a thumb in Linc's direction.

"He lives here. You, on the other hand…"

Adam leaned over and kissed her cheek. "I know I don't live here. But it serves you right for tempting me like this."

Jade only shook her head. "You have so lost the battle," she said wistfully.

Pulling back, Adam looked at her in question.

"We'll talk about it later," she told him.

"Hey, Adam. You're keeping pretty late hours now, aren't you?" Noelle asked with a knowing grin.

"Ah, if you ladies are finished, I'd like to take my wife to bed," Linc interrupted, putting a hand around Jade's waist.

Adam smiled at Noelle, knowing that, too, would be a conversation for later. But he couldn't let all that concern him, either. What he was concerned with was the woman now standing on the other side of the couch, her blue silk robe pulled tightly around her body. A body he was having a difficult time sleeping at night without thinking about.

"We weren't finished but since we've been interrupted we'll have to pick up where we left off tomorrow. Right, Camille?" Jade asked with a huge grin.

Camille fumbled with the belt on her robe, then found Jade's gaze and smiled back. "Right. We'll continue tomorrow."

Noelle clapped. "That sounds like a plan. And since I'm the only one without a guy I'm heading to bed first. Good night all," she said, then disappeared from the room.

Linc looked over at Adam. "Shall I expect to see you at breakfast?"

Adam looked at Camille and shook his head negatively.

"Then good night to you. And, Camille, it's good to see you again."

Camille nodded to Linc. "Same here. Good night, Linc."

They were alone.

Adam, who hadn't thought past seeing her again, was now at a loss for what to say or do. She looked stunning. That tone of blue perfectly accented her mocha skin. Her chin-length hair had been pulled back into a loose knot. She stood close to the couch as if she didn't really belong here. He took a step toward her and she took one backward.

He paused. "I'm glad you came," he said slowly.

She shrugged and walked around the couch to stand at the end of the sofa table. "Jade's really nice. I didn't want to turn her down."

"You looked like you were enjoying yourself when I walked in."

"I was," she said quickly then cleared her throat. "Do you normally show up at people's houses at this time of night?"

Adam took off his jacket and laid it on the chair in front of him. He took this opportunity to move a little closer without seeming as if he were moving closer. "This is my brother's house."

"I know that but it's just weird that you're paying him a visit at this hour."

"I'm not here to visit him," he said and was finally standing just a few feet away from her. "I'm here to visit you."

Nervously she licked her lips. "You could have waited until morning."

He shook his head. "No. I couldn't."

For a minute they both stood still, then Adam took another step close to her. "I need to touch you, Camille. It's been a week since I've touched you."

He watched as her eyes closed and she took steadying breaths. When he'd left her in L.A. she'd been like putty in his hands, kissing and touching him as if she were going to miss him every bit as much as he was going to miss her. Apparently something had happened in the last week to change her comfort level. And Adam knew what that meant. "It's okay, Camille. Just keep on breathing. Nothing's wrong with you being here."

Camille shook her head but kept her eyes closed. This wasn't like her other attacks, she seemed to have some control this time. With her eyes closed he was able to approach her and just as he'd admitted, touched his fingers to her cheek. "What's the matter, baby?"

She opened her eyes slowly and seemed to take a moment until they focused on him. "There was another article. I saw it a couple of days ago. It said I was giving you and Linc personal favors to model for me."

Her words were spoken softly, matter-of-factly, and they enraged him. "What? What paper was that?"

"Vegas Today," she answered. "I know that the picture of you and that woman was old but it bothered me."

He cupped her face and kissed her forehead, then the tip of her nose. "I'm sorry that you were upset by an article. Not that I have any idea how you would get a Las Vegas paper in L.A., but that's not the point. What else did the article say?"

"It alluded to the doubts I was already having about not being your type," she said in a tone that Adam couldn't quite decipher.

"To hell with reporters and their papers!" he yelled, then expelled a deep breath. It angered him that she was even reading those papers, let alone relating to what they were saying. "If it'll make you feel better I'll call my lawyer."

"No." She shook her head adamantly. "Don't do anything. If you sue them it'll look like what they were saying was true."

His hands were in her hair raking through the thick mass until the elastic that had been holding it together fell to the floor. "You don't believe what they're saying is true, do you?" He searched her face, looking for some clue as to what she was thinking. She was no longer regulating her breathing nor was she trying to get away from him. In fact, she seemed eerily calm.

"I believe that it may be their opinion that we are an odd couple."

Adam was sure he visibly relaxed. "And what's your opinion on us as a couple?"

She continued to stare at him until Adam felt as if she were tearing apart layer by layer of him.

"I said I was willing to give this a go and I still am. I know that people won't like it. I'm trying to get used to that because I realize it's none of their business."

"Wow." Adam sighed.

"Wow, what?"

"Hearing you talk like this is different." She tried to look away. "Different in a good way."

"I'm not used to being in the public eye this much, but Dana says I should get used to it because even without you I'm pretty famous."

Adam chuckled. "Dana's right. And that's the lure. Two famous people getting together—imagine the likelihood of that working out." The words were out of his mouth before he could stop them. Was he thinking that this thing between him and Camille was something to work out? The fact that Kim had resurfaced more than confirmed his stance of never getting seriously involved again. Not to mention the increase in press he and Trent were receiving now that one of the Triple Threat Donovans had gotten hitched. Still, there was something about this woman.

She laughed and he pulled her closer for a hug. "I really missed you."

Camille sighed, wrapping her arms around his waist finally. He'd said he couldn't wait to touch her. Well she'd been feeling the same thing. The moment he'd entered that room her senses had gone on alert. Her body reacting solely to his closeness until she couldn't wait for Jade, Linc and Noelle to leave the room. All week she'd thought of the kisses they'd shared and how wonderful they made her feel. And now she couldn't wait until his lips met hers again.

"I really missed you, too," she admitted.

Adam pulled back and looked at her for a fleeting moment before capturing her mouth in a heated exchange. His tongue tangled with hers, sucking and pulling her into an abyss of pleasure. Her hands gripped his shirt, moved upward to feel the flexing of the muscles in his back.

He deepened the kiss and she moaned into his mouth. She tried to move closer, to be as close to him as humanly possible as they stood in the den of the woman's house she'd been invited to for the weekend. Camille felt wanton, brazen and sexy. Things she'd never felt before. His hands grasped her bottom and for a moment she was shocked. He had partially undressed her in the living room at her house, so this intimate touching shouldn't have bothered her. And actually, it didn't. It aroused her.

His mouth was hot as it moved over her jaw and down her neck. She heard him mumble her name and felt waves of heat swarming through her, accumulating at her center. His tongue was driving her wild, tracing paths of what could only be described as delicious licks of fire over her skin. He was now cupping her bottom so thoroughly that she was lifted from the floor. In a motion she'd only seen on television he swung her around and sat her on top of the sofa table. His fingers were quick to undo the belt of her robe and push the satiny material down until it pooled around her waist.

Camille spread her legs and welcomed him when he stepped between them, his fingers instantly going to the straps of her nightgown. In a flash her upper body was bare, her chest heaving as he stared down at her.

She bit her bottom lip, wondering what he was thinking as he looked at her nakedness. He sucked in a breath then reached out both hands as if he intended to cup her breasts. Instead he paused so close to touching her the heat from his hands circled her nipples. She shifted and was about to pull the nightgown up when he stopped her.

"No." Sucking air through his teeth he looked at her. "You are so beautiful."

Camille looked away and felt his fingers on her chin turning her back to face him. "It's true. From your personality to your—" his eyes lowered and he licked his lips "—your stunning body, you are beautiful."

She couldn't speak. Never had a man told her she was beautiful. She'd had dates in which they were either enamored with her success or her connections, or even in the hopes of getting her father to review their screenplay, but never were they this focused on her, or her looks.

"Now, don't move," he instructed.

He really didn't need to tell her that, she couldn't move right now if her life depended on it.

Adam lowered his head, taking one heavy breast into his palm and squeezing gently. He moaned and Camille arched her back. He squeezed again, letting the nipple poke through the opening of his hand and she gasped. He flicked his tongue over the puckered nipple and she cried out. Then he opened his mouth taking as much of the mound in as possible, sucking as if he depended on her for nourishment. Her fingers went to his shoulder, sinking into his taut flesh as he continued to suckle her. Between her legs moisture pooled and dripped until she felt dampness on her inner thighs. She tried to pull her legs together but his body was like a blockade.

He moved to the next breast and Camille's legs trembled. She knew that he'd felt that movement and experienced a moment of embarrassment. That moment quickly passed when Adam's mouth moved from her breasts to her stomach. Despite the growing desire Camille felt a prick of panic. Besides her thighs, her stomach was her least favorite body part. However, Adam didn't seem to notice as he was continually kissing and laving her skin. He pushed the nightgown up so that it now went around her waist like a satin belt, and lowered his head.

Camille might be a virgin but she knew about the intimacies between man and woman. She grasped his shoulders, attempting to push him back. "Adam," she whispered.

"Don't move," he growled and she stilled.

His tongue stroked her once and she felt like a domino tower wavering at a sudden breeze. He licked her again and she knew she was about to tumble.

Her scent was intoxicating, luring him, seducing

him. His fingers parted her folds and kissed her deeply, desirously, loving the feel of her warmth against his face. She must have put her palms down on the table, leaning back to leverage herself, because her center lifted, cupping his face as if to feed him better.

He ravaged her, dipping his tongue in and out of her center, loving the soft moans she emanated. His mind was so full of her, so focused on what she was doing to him until he'd almost forgotten where they were. And then her thighs quaked and tightened around his head and even that thought disappeared.

Adam was more than gentle as he slipped the straps of her nightgown back onto her shoulders and helped her down from the table. When she opened her mouth to speak he touched a finger to her lips then retrieved her robe and motioned for her to put her arms into the sleeves. When her back was to him he slipped his arms around her waist and pulled her back against him.

"We will finish this. Just not here," he whispered into her ear.

She lay back against him, letting her head rest on his shoulder. "I've never done…that before. It was wonderful."

"That was only the beginning of what I plan to do to you." She could hear the smile in his voice and was touched by the ease in which they'd shifted from their heated exchange. She supposed it was due to the fact that she still felt his warmth, which was now coupled by the stiff length pressed into her back.

"That gives me something to look forward to," she said in a much lighter tone than she'd felt when she'd first arrived in Vegas.

Adam turned her to face him and tweaked her nose. "But now I have to go before Linc comes down here and throws me out."

"He wouldn't do that," she argued. "Would he?"

Adam chuckled then released her to pick up his jacket. "Linc knows me very well. He's not going to get one ounce of sleep knowing that I'm under the same roof as you. And he takes his rest very seriously."

Camille slipped her hand into his and began walking toward the door. "I see."

They were near the front door when Adam said, "Make some time for me tomorrow night."

"I don't know. Jade has lots of things planned for us and I think I'm meeting your mother for lunch."

"Tell Jade you have a date. She'll understand." He cupped her faced and kissed her thoroughly. "I'll pick you up at eight."

Camille smiled, loving the feel of his tongue against hers. "I'll tell her but I don't know if she's going to like it."

"I'll deal with the backlash," he said and was gone, leaving Camille with the memory of one fantastic orgasm.

Chapter 10

"He's not what I thought," Camille said as she and Jade sat in the sunroom eating bagels and sipping coffee.

"I don't think the Donovan men are what anybody expects. People tend to see only what's on the outside. Then they make assumptions." Jade broke a blueberry bagel in half and lifted her knife to smear on some cream cheese.

"I've always wondered why that is. Why is it that some people feel they have the right to judge?"

"Because they have nothing better to do," Jade said after swallowing a bite. "The key is not to give those types of people too much of your time. It's not worth it. Besides, you can't change their minds." She took a sip of coffee. "Take Linc for example. He was the head of the Triple Threat Donovans, the oldest and most devout bachelor. When he started seeing me there was talk about me using him to get my spa off the ground. Then there were the rumors of Linc paying off a debt by marrying me. It was never-ending. And even now that we've been happily married for almost a year they still write stupid articles predicting things like the demise of our marriage and the disfiguration of our kids."

"Are you serious?"

"I'm afraid so. It doesn't stop and there's not much we can do. Something about the First Amendment and all that bull."

Camille chuckled and chewed on her cinnamon raisin bagel. She rarely ate bagels because they were wasted calories so she chewed slowly, totally enjoying the taste of this one. Last night she'd eaten a brownie at Jade's insistence and hadn't thought about it until just now. She took another bite of her bagel.

"So when are you going to sleep with him?" Jade asked out of the blue.

Camille choked on the last bit of bagel. Jade only smiled as Camille cleared her throat and because she was thinking that maybe she'd made a friend in Adam's sister-in-law, she smiled in return. "What makes you think I haven't already?"

"Um, let's see. The fact that he showed up here after midnight to see you. And the fact that you were up bright and early this morning, making coffee when, if you would have done like I would have and made love to him in the den, you would have still been fast asleep."

"Well," she started to say. "I guess you have a small point there. It's complicated."

"Love usually is."

"I'm not in love."

Jade nodded. "Yup, and I'm not sitting here drinking the best damn cup of coffee I've ever tasted."

"And neither is Adam."

"Don't underestimate Adam. He's very intelligent and not nearly as pigheaded as his brothers."

"Love is not in our future," Camille said, then wondered at the truth of her words. She really liked Adam, and after last night she had the impression that he really liked her. But really liked was not love.

"What if it is love? Are you against that?" Jade lifted her napkin to her mouth and wiped. "You sound like you're trying to convince yourself that it's not possible."

Contemplating Jade's words Camille sat back in her chair and looked out the window to the bright sunlight. "I'm actually trying to keep myself from being too disappointed when whatever Adam and I are doing ends."

"I used to live my life waiting for the next bad

thing to happen, too. And believe me, a lot of bad things occurred before I finally decided it was time to enjoy all the good stuff that happened in between. I heard about your father. Does that have any bearing on how you perceive things with Adam?"

Camille lifted her cup of coffee and continued to stare out the window. They had a terrific view of the golden desert and the tops of hotels along the strip. There was no question that they lived in Las Vegas, but Las Vegas did not intrude into this house.

"I loved my father very much. Next to Dana, he was my best friend. He tried to be understanding of things I was going through growing up." She trailed off, thinking that what the therapist had told her was true. She should have told her father how Moreen treated her, the things she'd said to her when her father wasn't around. But she'd known her father loved Moreen and she hadn't wanted to hurt him. Instead she had resigned herself to endure Moreen's treatment for the sake of her father's happiness. It had never occurred to her that he wouldn't have wanted her make that sacrifice. "When my father died I felt…I don't know, betrayed."

Jade nodded knowingly. "Yup, that's just how I felt when my grandmother died. She'd been taking care of Noelle and I for so long there was never a thought of her not being there. And then one day she was gone. I couldn't believe it. I wanted to hate her, and yet I loved her so much living on seemed impossible."

"That's just how I felt."

"But I did have to live on. And so do you. I'm sure your father wouldn't want you going through life waiting for the other shoe to fall."

"He always said I needed to find peace with myself first before I could be truly happy. In the last few weeks I've thought a lot about him saying that and how it might be true."

"I think your father had a very good point. I also think that you and Adam have a brighter future than you're willing to admit. He's a good guy, Camille. And I'm not just saying that because he's my brother-in-law."

Camille set her cup down and turned to Jade. "If he's such a good guy, then what does he see in me?"

"My mother called you a gem," Adam said when they were seated in his car that evening.

"Wow, I've never been called a gem before." Camille stared straight ahead, her mind racing with thoughts. Her conversation with Jade this morning had left her thinking about her father and finally feeling a small sense of peace at his passing. It also made her think about Jade's words that just so happened to match Adam's.

"You underestimate yourself, Camille. Stop doing that," she'd said.

And as she'd showered and dressed Camille realized that they were both right. She did underestimate herself. After staring into the mirror for a few minutes she admitted that she had a pretty face. Yes, her cheekbones were high and her cheeks just a little bit chubby, but she was not hard to look at. She'd slipped into her jeans and shirt and stood at the full-length mirror behind the bathroom door. She was not as wide as a train, as Moreen had so often told her. Turning to the side she saw a very round bottom and even rounder breasts. Smoothing her hand down her belly, she noted that it wasn't as bad as it could have been. In fact, in these jeans it actually seemed a little flatter. No, her jeans weren't tight, but rather they fit her curvy size perfectly.

So when she'd returned to the Donovan living room it was with a little more self-confidence and a lot more excitement. She and Jade were having lunch with Mrs. Donovan and Camille actually found herself looking forward to it.

Lunch had been more than pleasant. Beverly Donovan was a striking woman, both in looks and personality. She'd instantly hugged Camille upon meeting her, then proceeded to talk about everything from clothes to what she was planning to serve for dinner tonight. The three of them spent two and a half hours together and Camille couldn't remember the last time she'd had so much fun. For a moment she'd felt as if she had a mother and a sister.

Afterward Camille had taken a nap, and rose just in time to take a bath and get ready for her date with Adam. Jade had been more than understanding when she'd announced that he was coming to pick her up. And since she'd mentioned it while they were at lunch, Mrs. Donovan hadn't wasted a moment telling her that she and Adam made a good couple.

So as she sat in his car now she was very happy to be with him, but filled with so many new revelations she didn't quite know how to categorize them all.

"It means she likes you," Adam was saying. "She definitely likes that catalog you left with her. I'm sure you'll have another huge order by the time you get home."

For some reason that thought didn't make Camille happy. Tomorrow evening the Donovan jet was going to take her back to L.A., and Monday morning she'd be back in her office, staring out at the busy street wondering when she'd see Adam and his family again.

"Are you okay, Camille?" Adam asked suddenly.

"Hmm?" she said absently, then turned to face him. "I mean, yes. I'm fine." Because he didn't look as if he believed her she reached out and rubbed his arm. "I'm fine. Where are we going?"

Adam stared at her for a moment then said, "I'm taking you out to dinner, remember?"

"Oh, yeah." She did remember but had just

thought of something else she'd rather do. "Why don't we go to your place instead?"

Adam's head jerked as he looked at her this time. "What? My place?"

"Yes, Adam. I'd like to see where you live." She smiled. "Unless you don't want to share that part of yourself with me."

"Don't be smart. I don't have any secrets from you. I just didn't think you would want to… I mean, I didn't know if after last night you'd still want to…"

Camille put her hand on Adam's thigh. "I want to go to your house."

Adam had no idea why their plans had changed but wasn't particularly upset that they had. Twenty minutes after Camille's request was made they pulled into the garage at his apartment building. After parking the car he went around to let Camille out, taking her hand and pulling her close to him as he did.

"Just so you know, I don't bring women to my apartment," he said when they were standing against the car.

Camille blinked as if in shock. "Really?"

He brushed her hair back from her face and nodded. "Really."

"Then where do you…ah… I mean, where…" she stammered.

"Vegas has a multitude of hotels." He grinned, then took her hand and walked toward the elevator.

He opened the door and watched as she walked inside. The layout put her in the middle of the living room, and he leaned over to turn on a lamp so she could see. She moved through the room looking around, touching a picture of his parents on the coffee table then sighing as she ran her hand over one of the huge suede pillows on the sofa.

"Can I get you something to drink?" he asked, thinking to himself that if he was going to have to watch her walking around his apartment in those tight-fitting slacks and even tighter turtleneck he was going to need all the help he could get.

When she'd entered the living room at Linc's house where he waited for her earlier this evening he'd almost swallowed his tongue. She looked absolutely edible in the apple-green pants and matching top. Her beige boots had a spiky three-inch heel on them and should have been illegal for the way they emphasized her calves.

"I'm not thirsty," she said in a voice that was way too sultry.

He instantly turned away. "I am." Moving to the bar in the corner of the room he poured himself a brandy, choosing that over the really hard liquor, which he was afraid he probably needed more. How was he supposed to keep his hands off of her if they were alone in his apartment? That's why he'd been glad they were going to a restaurant for dinner.

He emptied the contents of his glass then turned,

ready to face her again. Except she was directly behind him so when he turned they collided. She stumbled back and he instinctively reached out to grab her to keep her from falling. His hands fitted around her waist, his fingers splaying over the top of her buttocks.

Her palms flattened on his chest and they both laughed.

"Maybe you shouldn't indulge in another drink, Mr. Donovan," she said with a smile that could only be construed as coy.

Adam blinked in surprise. Camille being coy. That was definitely new. "Maybe we should have a seat," he said, removing his hands from her body and walking toward the couch.

He sat down and looked up to see her approaching. When he thought she was going to sit beside him she stepped between his legs and leaned over him instead.

"Are you nervous, Adam?" she whispered, so close to him that he could feel the warmth of her breath on his face.

He closed his eyes, took a deep breath, inhaled the floral scent of her perfume and felt his body fill with heat. "No. I'm not nervous."

"Then why don't you kiss me?"

"I didn't know you wanted to be kissed."

For a moment she looked startled. Then she smiled. "I always want to be kissed. By you."

He had no idea what had changed with her and

wasn't about to complain. While the Camille he was used to had a quiet demeanor this one was a pleasant shock with her blatant sexuality. Whatever her personality profile, at the end of the day she was a woman and he was a man.

So the fact that he reached up, grabbing her by the back of her head, and pulled her down until his lips felt hers should have been expected. When she opened her mouth in response, her tongue dipping languorously into his mouth to capture his, he knew that it was more than expected. She had demanded this response from him and while he had no clue why, again he wasn't about to complain.

She took the kiss deeper, pushing him back until he lay on the sofa, then climbing on top of him. His hands went to her bottom, cupping the voluptuous mounds and she began to pump. Heat swirled through his body until he thought he would explode from the intensity. Every brush of her center over his engorged sex made him dizzy and thankful of the fact that he was lying down.

Her breasts moved over him, a wicked entice-ment that he cursed. Her hands moved over his shoulders, down his torso and were now pulling his shirt from his pants. She seemed impatient, frenzied in her movements until her hands touched the skin of his stomach. Then she stilled, only her tongue moving inside his mouth. Adam wasn't sure what she was thinking but knew that between her kisses and her touch he was on his way to heaven.

After a few moments Camille moved her hands, slowly, tortuously, over his abs, up his sides then rested one on each pectoral. Following her lead he slipped his hands under her sweater, feeling the bare skin of her back. When she tore her mouth from his to nip his jawbone he breathed, "Camille, baby, what are you trying to do to me?"

She pulled back, looked down at him and smiled. "I'm returning the favor from last night."

Adam's eyes rolled back in his head. If she for one minute thought she was going to do to him what he did to her, he was definitely in trouble. "Ah, wait…wait a…minute," he said, trying to talk as she pushed his shirt up and over his head. His chest was bare now and she didn't waste a moment bending her head and capturing his nipple between her teeth.

He hissed. Then moaned as her tongue flattened over the spot.

"Camille." Her name was a deep-throated growl that seemed to spur her on.

Lower and lower her busy little mouth and tongue moved until her fingers traveled to his belt buckle, deftly undid it and unbuttoned his pants. He heard his zipper being lowered and grabbed her shoulders.

"Camille!" He shook her slightly, intent on stopping her before she did something she would regret. Although he was sure he would absolutely love it, he wasn't so selfish as to allow her to go this far without understanding what it meant.

"What? Am I doing something wrong?" she asked.

Her eyes had grown larger, her mouth, swollen from their kisses, looked delectable. Adam sat up, keeping her comfortably on top of him. "No, baby, you're not doing anything wrong. I just want to make sure you know what you're doing."

She looked down at her hands, then away toward the other side of the room. "You're right. I don't know what I'm doing. But if you just tell me I know I can make you feel good."

He'd been in denial since the first time he'd kissed her. He'd fought it and chalked it up to this business deal or anything else. But at this precise moment, looking into her warm brown eyes, seeing her worrying, her embarrassment coupled with her desire to please him, he knew all was lost. He was in love with this woman.

"That's not what I meant," he said softly, brushing his fingers over her lips. "Are you ready for this, Camille? Because I guarantee you that if I let you proceed there will be no turning back. I want you so badly I'm on the brink of exploding right here, right now. So you've got to be absolutely sure."

She nodded, then eased her tongue out to lick his finger. "I'm positive."

With those words Adam didn't waste another minute. Standing, he held her in his arms and walked to the bedroom.

He sat her on the bed and kissed her long and lovingly. She reached for his pants again and he moved her hand away. "Not yet. I won't survive if you touch me right now."

Instead he began to undress her, loving each feel of her flesh against his hands as he did. When she was naked he moved her to the center of the bed and looked down at her. All the curves he'd seen through her clothes were exemplified. Her mocha skin almost sparkled and his mouth watered. "I told you before you were beautiful." He shook his head. "But now, that word does not seem to do you justice."

She reached her hands up to him and whispered his name. Adam reined in his raging hormones and said, "Undress me, Camille."

She sat up on the bed and pushed his pants down over his hips. When he climbed off the bed to step out of them he noticed her watching him. She scooted to the edge of the bed then pushed his boxers down and again watched him as he stepped out of them.

"Now, touch me," he said through clenched teeth.

Tentatively Camille wrapped her fingers around his length. When he was cupped in her hands he sucked in a breath. "Stroke me."

She did and Adam felt the room tilting around him. "Camille," he whispered and closed his eyes.

He was enjoying the feel of her hand moving

over him, loving the attention she paid to what she was doing and all but ready to push her back on that bed and sink inside of her when he felt warmth over his arousal.

He cracked his eyes and wished he'd kept them closed. Her head was lowered and in the next instant her mouth was on him. His heart stood still, then hammered. Adam felt like screaming, every muscle in his body had grown taut. Instead he focused on breathing, on keeping calm until she was through. He had no doubt that this was her first time doing this, just as it had been her first time on the receiving end last night. Just as what they would do next would also be her first.

Her movements were tentative at first then increased to a rate that had him seeing stars. Of their own accord his hands rose and fisted in her hair. His teeth clenched and his breathing grew labored. On that final shaky breath he pushed her away and climbed on top of her. In his mind he knew that this was her first time and that he should go slow, but his body wanted total dominance, total satisfaction. He quickly pushed her legs apart, got a glimpse of her moistened center and shook.

To clamp down on his own arousal he only had to look into her eyes. They were dulled by desire, etched with expectancy. He leaned forward and kissed her forehead, the tip of her nose and finally her lips.

"I want you to relax and trust me," he said, his lips

a whisper from hers, his fingers moving to her center.

Camille gasped then nodded. Her goal had been clear: make love to Adam tonight, no questions and no regrets. She would be returning home tomorrow, returning to her normal, business-as-usual, boring life. She wanted for once to experience something else. She wanted to take a piece of Adam back to L.A. with her.

His finger moved slowly inside of her, back and forth until she could hear the sound of her moisture on him. He kissed her, his tongue parting her lips slowly and pushed another finger inside of her. She moved her hips, wanting more of the sweet sensations rippling through her body.

Withdrawing his fingers from her center he spread the moisture over her labia, upward to touch the hood of her and back down to the center again.

She murmured his name over and over again, unable to do or say anything else. Then he lifted from her, reached over to the nightstand and produced a condom. He quickly sheathed himself then settled between her legs once more. She spread them wider in an effort to show him that she was more than certain, that she wanted this more than anything else in the world.

The tip of his hardness settled over her opening and she tensed, sucking in a breath.

"No," he whispered, "keep breathing. Take long, deep breaths."

She did as he said and felt her body relaxing.

"Keep your eyes on me," he said and she felt him pushing against her.

It felt as if he wouldn't fit and her fingers fisted in the sheets. She closed her eyes and heard him telling her to open them. She did, looking deeply into his eyes and feeling a connection beyond anything she could have ever imagined.

"Just a little more and then it'll be okay," he said and pushed his length farther inside her.

Camille gasped with the brief moment of pain. Above her Adam stilled, showering her face with kisses.

"Thank you. Thank you," he whispered over and over again.

Instinctively Camille wrapped her arms around his neck, lifted her legs and clasped them behind his back, then she moved her hips.

"Mmmm," he moaned and began stroking, slowly with her.

Camille felt something building in her center, a ball of fire, growing, causing her to move her hips faster. Adam gripped her hips, tightly holding her as he moved deeper and deeper inside her.

This feeling was supreme. Pleasure she couldn't quite describe. Their bodies joined at the center, locked into a mating dance that seemed beyond natural. Her heart swelled with emotion, although she didn't dare name that emotion. Each time his fingers touched her it was with a gentleness that almost made her cry. And when he impaled his length in her, it was with slow deliberateness designed to make her beg.

And that she did when that fire had grown inside of her and now felt as if it were a volcano about to explode. She couldn't hold on; her breath hitched, her head thrashing against the pillow. For a minute she felt she was losing control, almost as if she was having one of her panic attacks. But this was different, this was propelled by pleasure and not fear or worry.

Adam lifted one of her legs, propping it up on his shoulder, thrusting deeper into her and she cried out. He filled her completely, moving with smooth precision and pushing her carefully over the brink.

With another thrust she fell, her limbs slackened while she panted, wondering why she'd waited so long for this type of pleasure. He whispered in her ear, "I love you, Camille."

He'd said it and he probably shouldn't have. No woman believed first confessions of love in the heat of the moment.

Still his hips moved above her, his length buried to the hilt inside of her. She was so warm, so tight, so wet and so accommodating. She gripped him until he was sure that she would drain all the life from him. And yet, he continued to pump, without another choice actually.

The fact was he did love her and even beyond that he loved the way it felt to be inside of her. How could he ever let her return to L.A. after this?

That decision along with that train of thought was taken out of his control as his entire body tensed, his climax taking over completely.

Chapter 11

Camille awoke in his arms. She was neither groggy nor tired as she usually was when she got up in the morning.

This morning she felt energized and ready to take on the world. Well, her thighs were a little sore, but it was a pleasant soreness. Visions of what she and Adam had shared last night materialized and she felt her body warming all over again.

It had been this way all night. All he had to do was touch her, brush a hand over her hip, or a kiss to her neck and she was on fire. Wanton was what most people would call it, but she didn't care. Over and over again he'd taken her and she continued to want more. Everything he did to her felt perfectly wonderful and while she had no one to compare him to, she was sure Adam was the very best lover in the world.

Gingerly she slipped out of the bed and made her way to the bathroom. Switching on the shower she waited while the water warmed. Just as she had every morning, every day of her life, she looked in the mirror. It was the same face she'd always seen and yet it was different. Her cheeks were flushed, giving her a mature glow that seemed to say, "I've had multiple orgasms." She smiled at the thought then looked down at herself. Her body looked the same but it felt totally different. She decided she liked the newness and stepped into the shower.

The water felt heavenly and she closed her eyes, arching her neck and turning so that it touched every part of her body. She continued to think of Adam and the words he'd said to her. Again he'd told her she was beautiful. As a matter of fact, he said those words each time he looked at her. Then he'd said something that she hadn't expected and didn't quite know what to do with.

He'd also said he loved her. At first she'd thought she was hearing things but when he'd reached his own climax he'd repeated it. And throughout the night he'd told her over and over again as if he were trying to get her to memorize it.

She shook her head and water from her hair splashed onto the tiles. Adam Donovan couldn't possibly be in love with her. Opening her eyes she reached for a bottle of shampoo that she'd spotted on an earlier trip to the bathroom. Lathering her hair she thought of his words and knew that if he said them, he most likely meant them. Adam didn't strike her as a liar. The question now was why.

Why would he choose her?

Then realization hit her. *Why wouldn't he choose her?*

She was just about to step beneath the spray of water again to rinse her hair but when she moved she bumped into a hard body. Attempting to turn around she was stopped by his hands in her hair. His long fingers stroked her scalp, massaging gently. Her entire body relaxed against him. From her scalp down to her toes her body tingled and she let out a soft moan.

He turned her to face him, pressing his hard length against her then backed her up until she was under the water. He rinsed her hair again, massaging her scalp, then his hands moved down to her neck and her shoulders.

In seconds he was palming her breasts, squeezing them until her nipples were turgid peaks. Over her belly his hands roamed. And since Camille had passed the self-conscious point about seven hours ago she focused totally on the pleasure of his touch.

His hand slipped between her legs as if it belonged there. He had an arm around her waist holding her steady. When his fingers entered her center she gasped, then began moving her hips against his motions.

Camille flattened her hands on his chest loving the feel of his taut muscles beneath her skin. Moving lower she felt his erection slick from the constant spray of warm water, already coated with a condom. She leaned forward, kissing his chest, stroking his length at the same time.

In the next instant she heard him moan. Then he lifted her. She wrapped her legs around his waist and he pressed her back against the tile, entering her as he did.

Again Camille was filled with him until her mind could think of nothing else. He pumped her with fierce strokes until, as if on command, she shattered in his arms. A few strokes later and he was groaning his own release.

They stayed that way for another minute or so before he lowered her to her feet. It was then that she opened her eyes and looked up into his. "Good morning," she whispered.

With a huge grin on his face Adam said, "A very good morning."

Jade hadn't seemed the least bit upset when Camille returned to her house way past noon. In fact, she and Linc had been sitting in the den when Camille and Adam arrived, and neither of them looked surprised that they'd spent the night together.

When she came back from changing her clothes

it had been decided that the four of them would spend the day together. Camille felt a moment's alarm as she'd been expecting her and Adam to spend as much time alone as they could before she left. However, Adam and Linc had already planned the day out and she couldn't bring herself to argue. Besides, they'd still be together.

Camille actually ended up enjoying herself as they'd toured Vegas. Because she was not a native she'd mistakenly been under the impression that the city was all casinos and lavish hotels. But the part they'd visited had great homes, big yards and scenery that put postcards to shame.

"Next time we'll do the official tour of all the casinos," Adam told her when they were on their way to dinner.

Camille only smiled, wondering when the next time would be.

They entered the Mandalay Bay and Camille looked at Linc with some confusion. "You're having dinner at the competitor's establishment?"

Linc smiled. "That's how I do most of my research."

Jade elbowed him in the ribs and Camille began to laugh with them.

The Mandalay Bay was a gorgeous hotel with its gold-and-cream décor. There was no evidence of the gambling since they'd entered through the Mandalay Place. Jade told her that they were having dinner at the r.bar.café.

"They have an excellent grilled Barramundi and I love the Cajun popcorn. Plus they have a bunch of shops we can peek into as we go."

"I don't know about the shops, I might be a little biased," Camille joked. She felt as if she'd known Jade all her life.

Jade laughed. "Don't worry, I am, too. But I was figuring if we go into some of the shops we could tell them who you are and maybe strike up some kind of deal."

"Oh no, there will be no deal. CK Davis Designs is going to open its own exclusive boutique at the Gramercy," Linc said.

Camille only stared at him. "I thought you just wanted to continue carrying some designs in the boutique you already have."

"I did. But I've been thinking that it'll be much more effective if it were an exclusive shop. I know you don't have one yet and this would be the first of many. What do you think?"

Camille didn't know what to think. She looked at Adam who had just given Linc a knowing nod and a smile. Then she looked at Jade who was grinning as if she'd known about this little announcement for some time as well. "I...um, I'm not sure. I haven't given much thought to opening my own stores. I've actually been content with mail orders. I mean, we've done well with mail orders."

Adam came to her side putting his arm around her. "Yes, you have. But just imagine how much better you'll do once you open stores across the country. You can start by hitting all the major cities. This is a great strategic move after the success of the fashion show. This way people won't have to wait to receive catalogs and then wait to receive their orders. They can just walk into the shop and buy the latest designs."

Camille listened to his words and thought how much they made sense. Her dream had been to simply design clothes and while she was an astute businesswoman she really hadn't given much thought to expanding beyond her Los Angeles home. But now, with the help of the Donovans, she was entertaining a whole other direction for CK Davis Designs.

"You might be right," she said slowly. "I'd have to research the market to figure out which cities would be best. Then I'd have to talk with my financial advisor to see how many I could start with."

"Okay, but right now we need to eat. I'm starving." Jade began walking toward the restaurant.

Camille shook her head. "I don't know how you stay so thin eating the way you do. I'd be as big as a house," Camille said then realized that her words, which normally would have made her think of her own size and eating habits and feel depressed, had come out as light as if she'd commented on the weather. She felt beautiful in her cream pant suit and each time she'd looked at Adam she'd seen him admiring her body with much appreciation. She could get used to this.

"In a couple of months I'll be big as a house but I've already decided I'm not going to worry about that until after the baby is born," Jade said nonchalantly.

Adam stopped walking. "After the baby is born? What baby?" He grabbed Linc by the arm. "What baby?"

Linc chuckled and Jade came to his side, entwining her arm in his and giving Adam and Camille a radiant smile. "We're pregnant."

Dinner was a celebration for all four of them and Camille had never had such a good time. So much so that going home had taken on a new low for her. But she held tight to her emotions as Adam drove her to the airfield. Her bags had already been loaded and the pilot said he was ready when she was. But she knew she wasn't ready.

"What's the matter? You look a little sad. I thought I was doing a pretty good job of entertaining you," Adam said as he held her loosely in his arms.

"I don't know." She shrugged. "It almost seems unfair that as soon as we take our relationship to another level we have to be separated. I kind of liked waking up with you this morning."

He leaned forward and kissed her lips quickly. "I really liked waking up with you. And I'm looking forward to doing it again in the very near future."

"How near?" she asked breathily.

"Thanksgiving is this week. The crew will be working around the clock for the first half of the week to get the wallpaper up and carpet installed. Then we'll only have to furnish the house. So I was thinking that I could come to L.A. and you and I could go to the house to do an inspection."

Camille tried to hide her disappointment at the fact that he was only thinking of seeing her again along business terms. "That sounds fine. I don't normally do much for Thanksgiving. Moreen wasn't the cooking type so she and Daddy preferred to going to restaurants."

"You spent Thanksgivings alone?" Adam asked incredulously.

"Not all of them. Sometimes I went with Dana to her parents' house. But now that she's married she'll have to divide her holiday time between her family and Carl's family. And I'll feel like a third wheel."

Adam nodded. "Then I guess I won't feel bad about what else I had planned."

"What else did you have planned?" she asked cautiously.

"I was thinking that after we did the tour on Wednesday we could head back here and you could spend the holiday with me. I mean, with me and my family."

Camille was elated. Her weekend with the Donovans had been very special. The eye-opening conversations with Jade, the warm reception she'd received from Mrs. Donovan and the crazy recitation

of Noelle's adventurous life, had been most entertaining and had contributed to her sadness about
leaving. Not to mention the step she'd taken with
Adam.

That could not be explained and while he hadn't
said anything about loving her again, Camille was
letting the idea that he really cared about her sink
in. It was a good feeling, that she mattered to
someone. A good feeling that Adam respected her
and defended her. If she gave herself a moment to
really think about it she would finally be able to
give her feelings for him a name.

"So what do you say?" he prompted when she
still hadn't answered him after a few seconds.

She smiled in response, then came up on tiptoe
and touched his lips with hers. "I think that's a fantastic idea."

Adam wrapped her tightly in his arms and
deepened the kiss. Camille felt as if there were so
much unsaid, yet felt through that intimate
exchange. He wasn't saying goodbye, but instead
conveyed "see you later" through the long strokes
of his tongue. When he nipped her bottom lip she
figured he was giving her a reminder of the things
he'd done to her with his teeth and tongue last
night. Her body warmed and she sank into the kiss,
conveying a few things of her own that she hoped
he'd pick up on.

As she slanted her head and opened her mouth
wider to him she wanted him to know that she'd

enjoyed all the things he'd done to her, that giving him her virginity was the best decision she'd ever made. Clutching the back of his head meant that she couldn't wait to be alone with him again and that she'd be thinking about him every second that they were apart.

The plane's engine was loud and disrupting, most likely what the pilot had intended, and Adam pulled away. "I meant what I said, Camille."

She stared at him in momentary confusion.

"I love you."

He released her then and Camille had no idea how her spongy feeling legs had gotten her onto that plane. But when she was belted in her seat she didn't have to think long about the word that described her feelings towards Adam Donovan. She loved him.

"As far as I can tell she left here and went to Europe. She got a few modeling gigs then moved in with some singer and got married," Trent said leaning back in his chair.

"So she's married?" Adam lounged on a leather couch. They were in the den at their parents' house, waiting for dinner to be served. Something they'd done since they were kids. While both he and Trent had their own homes, they didn't have a cook and they didn't have a hot meal on their table every night at seven. Which meant that at least four nights out of the week they were at their parents' house. "Why's she harassing me if she has a husband?"

"Had a husband," Trent corrected. "They divorced last year. She hung out overseas for a while longer then came back here two months ago."

"So what does she want?"

Trent shrugged. "Her bank account is far from zero so I can't say it's money. You said she says she wants to talk. Maybe that's all it is."

Adam shook his head. "No. I don't buy that."

"So what are you going to do?"

Adam thought about it for a moment then sighed. "Nothing."

"Nothing?"

"I have better things to occupy my mind with besides wondering about Kim Alvarez."

"Kim Alvarez? Now that's a name I haven't heard in a while," Linc said as he walked into the den and headed straight for the bar. "Why are we talking about her?"

Adam sat up in the chair and snatched a magazine from the table. "We're not. What are you doing here? Don't you have a wife and a kitchen?"

Linc emptied his glass. "Yes and yes. But one is pregnant, which means she's eaten us out of house and home already and hasn't had a chance to go to the market. So I'm here because I'd like a home cooked meal and one night without her scrutinizing everything on a take-out menu."

Trent laughed. "Oh the joys of family life."

"Jade's not that far gone in her pregnancy to be bothering you that much," Adam said.

"Then I invite you to come over to my house and stay a couple of days."

"She just had the sleepover with Noelle and Camille. She was fine then."

"That's because they're not the ones who got her pregnant," Linc swore. "One minute I'm the best husband in the world. The next she's cursing me because she can't stop throwing up or using the bathroom, depending on the time of day. I don't know if I can take seven more months of this."

By now both Trent and Adam were laughing until Linc shot them a scolding look.

"Hey, don't get mad at us, we're not the ones who got her pregnant," Trent said.

"Watch it," Linc warned and took another sip of his drink. "So why aren't we talking about Kim Alvarez?"

Adam stood, moving to the bar to fix himself a drink. "She's back in town and she wants to talk."

"To you? About what?"

Adam unscrewed the top from a bottle and poured into his glass. "I don't know and I don't care."

"Yeah, he was just about to tell me what other, more interesting, things are on his mind besides Kim and why she's here. Weren't you, Adam?"

Adam frowned at Trent, then spied Linc's curious gaze and took a long drink. "The house is almost finished. I have to take a trip to L.A. tomorrow."

"Isn't that convenient?" Linc quipped.

"Convenient? It's my job," Adam argued.

Linc gave him a knowing glare. "And I'll bet it doesn't hurt that Camille lives in L.A.?"

"So we're back to the alluring Ms. Davis," Trent said.

"No. We're not. I have to go to L.A. for business. Seeing as this business involves Camille I have no choice but to see her."

"And seeing as you're in love with her I guess that's a good thing," Linc added.

Adam looked at him then smiled. There was no use in lying; besides, he couldn't think of a reason that everyone shouldn't know how he felt about Camille. However, he braced himself for Trent's comments.

"A smile and no denial. Does this mean I've lost another brother?" Trent groaned.

Adam emptied his glass. "I haven't gone anywhere to be considered lost, Trent."

"But you're about to cross over to that married status aren't you?"

"No. I mean, I haven't asked Camille to marry me."

Linc took a seat across the room. "Are you going to?"

At that precise moment Henry Donovan stuck his head in the doorway. "Dinner's ready. Don't dawdle, you know how your mother is about being at the table on time."

Yes, Adam remembered quite clearly and couldn't resist thanking his mother for her timeliness. He was first out of the den, leaving Trent, Linc and their questions behind.

Adam had left his parents' house almost an hour ago but he was just arriving home. He didn't live that far from them but had stopped at the house he was finishing up for Ben to see how things were going. It was dark so he couldn't get a good idea of what had been done but then, that hadn't been his only purpose.

He loved this house, loved its shape and its feel. Secretly he'd hoped that Ben would change his mind and stay overseas for a couple more years, giving him the excuse to live in it for at least a short time.

And he'd also taken the opportunity to think more about his brother's words. Was he going to ask Camille to marry him?

It would seem the logical next step. But Adam hadn't thought about marriage in a very long time. And he wasn't sure he was ready to start now.

He was about to slip his key into the lock when he heard something behind him. He turned and came face to face with the only woman to ever break his heart.

"Hello, Adam. I figured I'd better come to you since you weren't in a hurry to see me."

Trent was right, she was a fantastic-looking

woman. Her golden skin had darkened a bit, her body certainly fuller in all the right places. Her eyes were still dark as night, her nose thin, her lips a neat little heart shape. Her ebony hair shone and hung over one shoulder.

"Hello, Kim."

"Is that all you have to say to me?" she said with a coy little smile that he remembered she used to break down all his defenses.

This time, years later, it didn't work. "Not really, I actually said everything I needed to say to you nine years ago, when you left me standing in an airport terminal."

Kim took a step closer to him. He inhaled and smelled her scent: pure sex. Another man would have hastily invited her inside. He folded his arms over his chest.

"That was a long time ago. I came to apologize. I was wrong."

Adam chuckled. "You were wrong to leave me for a career in modeling that you could have just as easily pursued here. Or were you wrong for leaving me to marry that singer? I get confused with all your lies and mistakes."

One elegantly arched brow rose and the corners of her lips lifted. "Keeping tabs on me, huh?"

"No. Trent checked you out. The same way he would a terrorist or any other criminal."

"Hmm, Trent still acting like the family James Bond?"

"Enough with the small talk. I'm going to bed," he said and turned his back to her, attempting to unlock his door again.

She pressed herself against his back, her hands going around his waist, her cheek lying against his spine. "I've missed you, Adam."

Adam turned and pushed her away. "You're crazy, Kim."

She stared at him looking half hurt and half pissed off. "You never were the type to hold a grudge, Adam. What happened to you?"

"You, happened to me." And she was right—he didn't normally hold a grudge but his gut instinct was telling him that there was definitely something else to her return to Vegas. "Why did you really come back, Kim? And don't tell me it was because you all of a sudden felt guilty and wanted to explain why you walked out of my life."

"I missed you."

"Wrong. I don't believe that, either." He took a step toward her then stuffed his hands into his pockets. "Look, the thing is if you did really come back to talk to me, don't bother. I've moved on and so should you. Whatever happened nine years ago is finished. Now, I'd like you to leave."

"I'm not leaving until you invite me in and we can talk," she said adamantly.

Adam shrugged. "Then you can stand out here all night." He turned and slipped his key into the door then looked back over his shoulder. "But if you're here in the morning I'm having you arrested." With that said Adam let himself into his apartment and slammed the door.

Camille couldn't seem to get a handle on the butterflies that had been dancing in her stomach since waking up this morning. She'd forgone her usual cup of coffee for fear the added caffeine would turn her into a blabbering basket case.

Now she paced her office, sketches of her latest designs in hand. As she walked she looked them over thinking of alterations, fabrics, colors. She was humming a tune to some love song she'd heard on the radio last night while she and Adam had talked. It was after eleven and she was anxiously waiting for him to arrive.

He'd said his plane would arrive around one and she knew she wouldn't breathe normally again until then. She couldn't wait to tell him how she felt about him. Each time they'd talked on the phone she'd thought about saying it but realized that over the phone wasn't going to cut it. She wanted to see his face, to watch him as he digested the fact that she loved him right back.

Again her stomach fluttered. The thought of her being in a committed, loving relationship was still a surprise to her, only now it was a pleasant surprise.

She was about to start singing aloud when there was a knock on her door and Sofari poked her head inside. "I know you said no more articles, but—"

Camille waved her inside. "It's okay. I'm not worried about words on paper anymore. Bring it on," she said, holding out her hand.

Sofari crossed the room and handed the newspaper to her. Sofari was out of her office before Camille could sit at her desk. That in itself was abnormal but Camille was too happy to question it.

So she sat back in her chair and placed the paper on her desk. Leaning forward she prepared to read.

The picture stopped her first. It was Adam in front of the door to his apartment with a woman plastered to his back. The woman was smiling while Adam's face was a silhouette.

Her heart took one long, slow pause then pattered quickly. She tore her eyes away from the picture to read the headline.

TRIPLE THREAT DONAVAN MOVES ON, OR SHOULD WE SAY MOVES BACK

Her throat clogged and she struggled to take a deep breath. Forcing her eyes to stay on the paper she began reading the article.

The infamous playboy, Adam Donovan, was spotted entering his apartment after a late night on the town with Kim Alvarez, an international model and former wife of Grammy Award winning singer, Dante Dominion. Donovan and Alvarez are said to be rekindling an old flame since they were once high-school sweethearts. Apparently, Donovan has gotten over the Fashion Diva and moved on to greener pastures.

Camille felt as if her entire world were spinning out of control. She sat back in her chair, letting her head loll and her eyes close.

Breathe, she told herself.

One deep breath. Images of Adam and her in Linc and Jade's den appeared.

Two deep breaths. Her body shivered with memories of Adam's kiss, his touch.

She thrashed her head, struggling, but finally making the third deep breath. Focus, take control, don't let the panic win. Over and over she told herself to remain calm.

Then she opened her eyes and saw the paper on her desk, the picture of Adam and this woman. Releasing a long, shaky whoosh of air Camille lifted the paper and dropped it into the trash. She opened her desk drawer and pulled out her purse. Standing, she walked across the room to the coat rack and retrieved her leather jacket. Opening the door she walked out, saying to Sofari as she passed her desk, "I'm gone for the weekend."

Sofari didn't have a chance to respond.

Chapter 12

Adam stepped out of the car and almost ran to the door of her building. He could barely wait for that last meeting with Max to be over so he could grab his bags and head to the airport.

He checked his watch and saw that it was fifteen minutes to one. He was on time and couldn't wait to see her. Walking purposely he was a bit annoyed when Sofari stopped him.

"Ah, Mr. Donovan?" she said.

"Yes," Adam answered in as calm a voice as he could.

"She's gone."

He stilled. "Who's gone? Camille?"

Sofari nodded. "Yes. About two hours ago she left for the weekend."

He brushed a hand over his hair. "I thought I was supposed to meet her here and we would go to the house together. Did she say she was going to her father's house?"

Sofari fidgeted with some newspapers then looked back up at him. "She didn't say."

Because she was making so much noise with the paper Adam's gaze fell to the desk. He saw the title of the Las Vegas newspaper and took a step closer to the desk. "May I?" he asked, slipping the paper from beneath Sofari's hands.

As he turned the paper around so he could read it, his heart plummeted and rage roared through his body. He threw the paper across the room then walked through the flying papers until he was back out on the street.

Getting back into the car he directed the driver to go to Camille's apartment at the same time pulling his cell phone out of his pocket.

"Trent Donovan."

"Yeah, it's me. Listen, I need you to find out who this reporter is at *Vegas Today* and why he's so hell-bent on reporting about me and my women all of a sudden."

"I'm fine and how was your trip, Adam," Trent said.

"I don't have time for this, Trent. I need you to get on this now!"

"Okay, calm down. What's going on?"

Adam told Trent about this article and the ones that had been printed recently. And while he was used to being in the news he'd never made headlines this many times within a month and sometimes, although they were few and far between, they actually reported on his business conquests as well as his love life. These recent articles seemed geared towards him and who he was dating.

Who he was dating? A thought entered his mind and he prayed it wasn't possible.

"You're right. It sounds strange. Especially with Kim being back in town and now she's in a picture with you. So I'll check on the reporter and find out who his sources are," Trent said finally.

"Yeah, she's definitely involved. I wasn't with her all night long. I went to Ben's after I left Mom and Dad's. She must have been waiting at my place. And if she was waiting, it's logical to assume the reporter was waiting, too."

"I'll check her out again."

"And check out Moreen Davis, as well," Adam said as a precaution.

"C'mon, Adam. I know she's a witch but do you think she'd go this far?"

Adam was afraid of what to think. All he knew was that Camille had seen this paper, this Las Vegas newspaper that once again had made its way to Los Angeles and to her office. She'd read this article and been pissed off. He couldn't say he blamed her but damn if he wasn't desperate to find her to convince her it was all lies.

Half an hour later Adam had banged on Camille's door for fifteen minutes and had called both her apartment and her cell a half dozen times. He'd finally given up and jumped back in the car headed towards her father's house. Taking out his cell phone again he called Dana.

"Hi, Dana. This is Adam Donovan. I hope I'm not disturbing you."

"No, Adam, you're not. How are you?"

"I'm fine. Listen, I'm trying to find Camille. Have you seen or heard from her?"

"I talked to her when I was at the office this morning. She said she was meeting up with you later and then you were going back to your parents' for the holidays. Is something wrong?"

Adam ran a hand down his face. "Yes. Something is very wrong."

"What is it? I'll be right there," Dana said tension rising in her voice.

"No," Adam said hastily. "It's not like that. I think Camille saw another article about me and is upset. I just left her apartment but I didn't get an answer. I'm wondering if she went to her father's place without me."

"I told her to stop believing everything she reads," Dana said.

"I know. I tried to tell her the same thing. But I

can see how this article may have really bothered her. I have to find her to explain."

"You really love her, don't you?" Dana asked out of the blue.

Adam didn't hesitate. "Yes. I do."

Camille arrived at the house at one-thirty. After leaving her office she'd gone home and packed. No, she wasn't packing for a weekend in Vegas with the Donovans but she was going to spend Thanksgiving someplace else.

Thinking as she drove she came to the conclusion that she was tired of having her life dictated by other people's actions. Since meeting Adam she'd been on an emotional roller coaster. And while the emotions she'd experienced with him weren't the tumultuous, self-condemning feelings she'd gone through her whole life with Moreen, it was still draining.

Could she be with a man with this type of reputation? Could she live her life wondering if this article as opposed to the last one were true? These were questions that made her heart rate increase, a panic attack slowly coming on.

But this time Camille calmed herself. Her father was no longer here and neither was Adam. It was time she got a grip on her own life, her own feelings. So as she drove, thinking about all that had happened in the last week, she kept her hands tightly on the steering wheel and chanted calming statements to herself. For the most part it worked because she hadn't passed out and she wasn't shaking uncontrollably. She did get really hot at one point and had to wind down the windows, but the fresh air worked wonders in bringing her around.

So as she pulled up in front of her father's house she thanked her therapist and realized that all the money she'd spent on her hadn't been a total waste.

The land surrounding the house had been re-landscaped so that in addition to the plush carpet of grass there were small shrubs lining the walkway. The walkway that used to be red brick but was now an interesting mosaic of gray stone. Once she got closer she saw that the new steps to the front door had been changed to that same gray stone with huge white urns filled with more lush greenery. The door that used to be wide and dark oak was now a double white door, with glass center panes. On the pane was an intricate gold design that was continued in the two skinny windows along-side the doors.

Reaching into her purse she found the key Adam's secretary had forwarded to her earlier in the week. She slipped it into the door and stepped inside. The foyer had been transformed from its dark cherry wood to an open and airy beige, cream and gold space. The floor was a beige marble with gold accents. Pedestals stood at perfectly spaced intervals but at this point did not have anything atop them. The staircase, as it had always been, was the focal point to the foyer and surprisingly had not been changed. It had however, been shined to a premium luster, so that the light oak railing gleamed.

Camille remembered traveling up and down those stairs on many occasions. She continued to move through the house noting the changes and feeling a sense of accomplishment. While she really hadn't had much to do with the project up until this point, it was clear that Adam and his company knew what they were doing. The house was the same and yet different. She felt the memories and yet they weren't as poignant as they had been when she'd come to the house months ago.

Her heart hammered but it wasn't in panic. She felt waves of excitement at what the finished product would look like and prickles of pride for Adam and his company.

She was upstairs in the room that used to be the master bedroom looking out over the new pool area when she heard a sound behind her. She turned and saw him and almost tripped over the four-poster bed that had been left there by the crew. She'd instructed Max at the last minute to have them keep that bed. She wasn't entirely sure why since she had a bed at her apartment but this one was a family heirloom she couldn't bear to part with.

He took a step forward and she quickly righted herself. The last thing she needed was Adam touching her. A part of her had known he would follow her but she hadn't given any thought to how she would handle that.

"What are you doing here?" she asked, knowing the question didn't make sense.

He looked as if he'd been through the wringer. His normally smiling eyes seemed shadowed, his broad shoulders slumping a bit. She resisted going to him, barely.

"You left me," he said in a quiet voice.

Her heart was pattering, not pounding. She was nervous but not in a state of panic. Was it the house or the man?

"I don't think I can do this, Adam." His name caught in her throat and she forbade herself to cry. For the last three days she could think of nothing more than how much she absolutely loved this man. And in the space of fifteen minutes a newspaper and a picture had crushed that.

He shook his head and crossed the room until he was standing on the other side of the bed staring intently at her. "You can do anything you want. Stop underestimating yourself."

That wasn't what she expected him to say. She expected him to immediately plead his case. But then again he probably didn't know she'd seen the paper. "I saw the article and the picture. If you wanted to go back to your ex all you had to do was tell me."

With smooth motions his hands slipped into his pockets. His leather jacket remained open showing the black sweater he wore beneath. His jeans fit his muscled thighs perfectly and her heart pattered at how good looking he was. No wonder the press and every other woman in the world loved him.

"I am not getting back with my ex. The picture was a set-up. A pretty elaborate one at that," he said absently.

"I don't want to compete with every woman in the world and to wonder every day if another article about you and me will hit the papers," Camille said honestly. "It's too hard and it hurts."

Adam nodded. "I would never want to hurt you. But I can't stop people's opinions any more than you can. I am who I am and unfortunately the press likes that. You are who you are and they like reporting about you, as well. What are we supposed to do, live our lives under a rock to get away from it?"

She looked away from him then because staring at him and keeping her distance was becoming too hard. "I know who I am," she said quietly.

"Then what they print shouldn't matter."

"It does when they print that you've returned to your playboy ways, leaving me in the lurch. Dammit, Adam! We were just together on Saturday and Sunday. This picture was taken on Tuesday. How do you want me to react? When it was a two-year-old picture I could digest that. But not this!"

"I want you to trust me."

His words, spoken so softly, yet so seriously, had her turning to face him again.

"I want you to trust what we have and keep that foremost in your mind. Do you think I would cheat on you? Do you think I would lead you on? Tell me, Camille, is that the type of man you think I am?"

He was moving around the bed by then, with slow, measured steps that didn't crowd her yet let her know that he was approaching with or without her consent.

"I...I don't know," she finally admitted. But that didn't ring quite true even to her own ears.

"You do know," Adam said. "You know that I've been nothing but honest with you. I've even demanded that you be honest with yourself. I'm not a stranger to you."

He was standing right in front of her now. His scent, his form occupying her space with such gentle dominance she could barely breathe. And yet, she felt perfectly calm.

"I love you."

Was it the words that were her undoing or the man that professed them?

"And I love you. That's why this is so hard for me. For years I've refused to expect anything from anybody for fear of being let down. I've accepted limitations placed on me as the norm. I've lived in a bubble protecting myself from hurt and harm but it still found me," she said in one breath. "What am I supposed to do now? How am I supposed to deal with this? With you?"

His hands were on her shoulders before the last word was out. "Breathe," he said simply.

And she did.

She stopped talking, stopped thinking about the issue at hand and breathed. His hands rubbed up and down her arms and she closed and opened her eyes.

"Now tell me you love me again," Adam requested.

She focused on him, on his deep brown eyes, his strong jawline, his slightly crooked nose. "I love you, Adam."

He smiled. "Now you kiss me."

She leaned in, lifted her face to his and realized he wasn't going to meet her halfway. So coming up on tiptoe she touched her lips to his. Just a gentle brush and then she prepared to pull back.

But Adam had another idea. Grabbing her by the waist his lips fused to hers sending sparks of desire crackling into the air. His tongue eagerly parted her lips and tackled hers. Hesitation wasn't even in her vocabulary. Instead Camille wrapped her arms around his neck, pulling him closer as she opened her mouth wider, sucking his tongue deeper.

Adam groaned, cupping her buttocks and pressing her against his throbbing erection. She rubbed her center into him and blood thumped in his ears. Picking her up he took a step then dropped her onto the bed, falling down on top of her.

Her legs spread willingly and he rubbed up and down their length, angered by the fact that she wore jeans. Cursing he lifted off of her and yanked his jacket off. She followed suit and pulled her shirt over her head. Hastily they both got rid of their clothes. Adam reached into his pants pocket and pulled out a condom before tossing the pants to the floor.

Camille snatched the packet from his hand and opened it. Keeping her eyes on his she sheathed him. Adam hissed through clenched teeth, her hand on his erection sending waves of heat throughout his already aroused body. Unable to think of anything else Adam lifted her legs, positioning her ankles on his shoulders and thrust deep.

"Adam," she whispered and he kissed her lips.

"Yes, baby." He rotated his hips, pushing deeper into her until he could go no farther.

She moved her hips and he thought he would lose it. Finding a pleasant rhythm Adam stroked her and stroked her until he was sure nothing in life had ever been this sweet. He would marry this woman, there was no doubt about that in his mind. He would make her his forever and then he'd deal with the reporters and this game they insisted on playing with people's lives.

Her legs quivered against him and he kissed her, capturing her screams of ecstasy. Grasping her ankles and spreading her legs wider he thrust into her once and felt his entire body shake.

He pulled back and thrust again. His world tilted.

And again, his heart plummeted. His body shook and release came in long glorious spasms.

Chapter 13

Although delayed by their lovemaking Adam and Camille still managed to tour the house, discussing designs and color schemes. By the time they boarded the Donovan jet late Wednesday night they had finally agreed on what the finished house would look like. And the designer could have it finished in the next two weeks.

Accordingly, Camille thought of what would happen when the house was finally finished. The house had brought her and Adam together. So while she would always love that house for the memories of her father, now she had a new appreciation for it.

It was after midnight when the limo stopped in front of Adam's apartment building. The door opened and she stepped out, stretching her tight muscles as she did. She was tired, both physically and emotionally. Today had been a very enlightening day.

Adam clasped her hand in his and led her through the door while the driver carried her bags in behind them. They were inside the apartment, walking into Adam's bedroom before he finally spoke.

"I think your stepmother has something to do with the articles," he said while taking off his clothes.

Camille had opened her suitcase on the bed and was looking through it to find her nightgown when she paused and looked up at him. "What?"

"I couldn't figure out why there was a sudden interest in you and me," he began. "I mean, the article after the fashion show was normal. Even the article about my past affair with the congressman's daughter wasn't totally out of the ordinary since whenever I'm not seeing anyone they tend to dig up old dirt."

He wore only his boxers now and the sight caused fresh spikes of desire to course through Camille. But now was not the time. She needed to hear where he was going with this. Closing her suitcase and setting it on the floor she began unbuttoning her own blouse. "I see."

"But the articles weren't just about me. They

were stabs at you, as well. Very personal stabs that knew just where to hit and when. Nobody else criticizes your appearance more than your stepmother. Am I correct?"

Camille hated to admit it. In fact, she hated to think of Moreen when she'd been having such a pleasant time with Adam. "Yes, you're right," she said finally.

He came to her then, helping her out of her shoes and jeans then slipping her nightgown over her head. His hands, as they seemed to do often, rested at her waist. "I know she doesn't like you. I picked up on that the first day we all met in my office. I'm inclined to believe it's jealousy but I know you don't see it that way."

"She's always hated me," Camille said quietly. "I don't know why. When Daddy first married her I tried to be extra good, to follow all her directions and to keep my room clean. But nothing I did was ever enough. She was always complaining."

Adam held her close. "The fault isn't with you, baby. It's with her and she knows that so she tries extra hard to make you as miserable as she is. You flipped the script when you offered your own deal then told her she could sell her share in the house then and there if she didn't like the deal. You finally stood up for yourself and she didn't like it. And at the fashion show you did it again."

Camille began to understand what he was saying. "So she wanted to get back at me. And what better way than to harass me the way she'd done all my life. That day in your office she told me I was silly for thinking that a man like you would be interested in me."

Adam ran his hands through her hair, then his fingers grazed her cheek. "She could tell that I was more than interested in you at that point. I think it was pretty obvious."

Camille chuckled. "To everyone but me, huh?"

He smiled. "You took a minute to come around. But now I think you're pretty confident in my feelings for you."

Camille wrapped her arms around him and rested her cheek against his chest. "I'm confident in our feelings for each other."

Adam kissed the top of her head and said, "Then we need to nip the wicked stepmother and her antics in the bud."

"Then let's do it," Camille said with conviction.

"It's Thanksgiving morning," Moreen complained the minute she entered the conference room of Donovan Investments. "Why I was summoned for this early meeting is beyond me. And unless you have a check with my name on it I'm going to be quite angry."

Max pulled out a chair for her. "Have a seat, Mrs. Davis. This meeting was a necessity and I apologize for any inconvenience it may have caused you."

Moreen harrumphed. "Lucky for you I was already here in Las Vegas."

Trent entered the room at those words and smiled at the woman. "Yes, very lucky indeed," he said menacingly.

With a wave of her hand and very little tolerance Moreen asked, "Who is he?"

"He's my brother, Trenton Donovan," Adam said when he came in holding Camille's hand. "I asked him here because he has information pertinent to this meeting."

Moreen frowned as Camille walked past her. Adam held out a chair for Camille and then they were all seated.

"Fine. Where's my check?" Moreen began.

Adam nodded toward Trent.

Trent cleared his throat then opened the folder he'd brought into the conference room with him. "Mrs. Davis, it is customary for Donovan Investments to do a preliminary background check on persons that it does business with."

"Please, get to the point. I have plans for the holiday," Moreen said.

"I wonder with whom," Camille mumbled.

Moreen shot her a seething glare.

"I found some pretty interesting things," Trent interrupted. "It seems your marriage to Randolph Davis was pretty hasty. You'd only known him for two months before you were married in a quiet ceremony at the Los Angeles courthouse."

"Is that a crime? Love at first sight works rather quickly," Moreen commented while surveying her nails.

"I'm not a believer in love at first sight," Trent said adamantly. "However, in further searching I found something that may have been the reason for the hasty nuptials. It seems you were seen at Cedar Sinai Hospital almost three weeks after the wedding. Old newspaper clippings reported a miscarriage while the hospital records reported food poisoning. Isn't that a strange discrepancy?"

"The records are wrong," Moreen said simply.

"Oh, the records are wrong but the press is correct. Okay. Since you take so much pride in the press always presenting the absolute truth, the reports of your many indiscretions during the years you were married to Randolph Davis are true, as well."

Camille gasped and Adam held tightly to her hand.

Moreen rolled her eyes. "Gracious, Camille, I really wish you would grow up. Randolph is dead. What I did while I was married to him is of no consequence to what is going on now."

"Oh, but it does," Trent said. "You signed a prenuptial agreement before marrying Randolph—he seemed to be a very smart man. In that agreement it specifically stated that if it could be proved that at any time during the marriage you were unfaithful you would receive nothing."

"That agreement was void the day he died."

"Maybe so, but Mr. Davis's attorney also had a letter from Mr. Davis dated two weeks before he succumbed to illness stating that he suspected you of cheating and that if it were true he was removing you from the will."

Moreen stood, slamming her palms down on the table. "This is insane! Like I said, Randolph is dead. Agreements and letters before that time have no bearing on the here and now."

"Except that there is now proof that you were cheating on your husband before he died."

The door to the conference room opened and in walked a very attractive young man. Camille could only stare because the man didn't look to be much older than her or Adam. She was momentarily confused. Adam had told her last night that Trent investigated Moreen and he'd told her that Trent had called just as they were leaving her father's house to go to the airport stating that he'd found everything he needed and they were meeting this morning. But Camille hadn't asked for any more details. She didn't want anything else to mar her time with Adam. Now she almost wished she'd known everything beforehand.

Moreen looked towards the door and gasped. "What are you doing here?"

Trent stood, walking to the door and shaking the man's hand before closing it again. "I'd like to introduce the world-renowned singer, Dante Dominion."

The name sounded familiar but Camille still couldn't place him.

"Mrs. Davis, surely you already know Mr. Dominion since you were having an affair with him for the last two years. In fact, your affair was what ended his marriage to one Kimberly Alvarez."

That's why his name was familiar. Camille remembered the article she'd seen yesterday morning and gasped, "What?"

"You can finish the story if you'd like, Mrs. Davis," Trent offered.

"This is ridiculous. I'm leaving." Moreen moved toward the door but Max stood blocking her exit.

"Fine. I'll finish it for you. About two months ago Kim Alvarez's divorce became final and she was going to collect half of everything Mr. Dominion owned. Mr. Dominion was very stressed by that. So Mrs. Davis, being so madly in love with her young beau, wanted to save her man from this misfortune. So she began selling any and everything Randolph Davis had left with her name on it to pay Ms. Alvarez off. She was almost finished with the payments when it came to the sale of the house.

"Camille foiled those plans when she suggested this new plan. That's when Mrs. Davis decided she needed to make Camille suffer. Mostly by coincidence she found out that Adam and Kim had been involved and came up with a perfect revenge. She offered Kim double the money to break Adam and Camille up. And to further secure this would happen, she planted those articles in the newspapers and made sure Camille would see them."

"How could you?" Camille said in a low tone. "Did you really hate me that much?"

Moreen looked at Camille. "You are so pathetic. You and your father both lived your lives with blinders on. I didn't love him any more than I liked being cooped up in that house with his whining daughter. I tried to convince him to send you away to school. Maybe I wouldn't have strayed so much if he'd done that. But he refused. So I figured to hell with both of you." She took a deep breath and stood up straight. "Again, I'll say that none of this changes the facts. I own half that house so when it sells I get a check."

"You don't deserve a dime of Randolph Davis's money," Adam said venomously.

Moreen gave him an impatient look. "That's your opinion. And personally I think your opinion and your choice of women sucks. Why you would pass up Kim for this I'll never understand."

Adam stood leaning over the table to glare at her. "Because Camille has more class in her fingernail than you and Kim combined. You're both opportunistic and calculating, something a man finds neither attractive nor alluring." Then he glanced at Dominion. "Unless the man is the same way himself."

Dominion jumped at Adam but was quickly put

in his place by Trent's large hands shoving him back into the chair.

Moreen threw her head back and laughed. "You are just as pitiful as she is. Fine. If you two want to be together I don't care. I just want my money."

"You won't get a dime," Adam said.

"Then I'll sue you and Donovan Investments and get triple the money," she argued.

It was Camille who stopped the exchange. Standing to walk around the table she stood in front of Moreen. "You didn't deserve my father and you don't deserve his money." She picked up her purse and retrieved her checkbook. "I'm buying you out of the house for half the price it was last quoted at and I'd suggest you take this check," she said as she scribbled, "and get as far away from me as you possibly can. Because if I see you again I won't be responsible for what I might do to you."

Moreen frowned. "Should I be afraid of the awkward little girl who's destined to get her heart broken again?"

"No," Camille said in a voice that was dangerously calm. "You should be afraid of the strong, self-assured woman who will kick your ass for all the pain and suffering you've caused her."

The room was totally silent, Moreen and Camille in a standoff as all eyes remained fixed on them.

"Don't underestimate me, Moreen," she said through clenched teeth, then dropped the check on the table in front of her stepmother and walked out of the room.

Camille was outside pacing, letting all the revelations that had just come to light travel through her system. The lies and the betrayal stung but the victory of standing up to Moreen outweighed that pain so that she felt liberated.

Then she paused.

She didn't know when Adam had come out into the hall and she didn't see him now. But she felt him. She felt his presence, his support and knew a greater love than she'd ever imagined.

Beverly Donovan set an amazing table. Camille had wandered into the dining room before the rest of the family. She looked down at the twelve-foot-long table covered in white linen and smiled. China and crystal dishes sparkled and candles were lit around the huge harvest-themed centerpiece.

The sideboard held several different wines and crystal pitchers of water and iced tea. Garland matching the table centerpiece was draped along the side adding to the holiday ambiance.

In the other room the Donovan family were having drinks and talking as families do. There was Mr. and Mrs. Donovan, Trent, Linc and Jade and Noelle. Max was there and his parents Everette and Alma, who she'd learned were related through Adam's father. And Ben had arrived home earlier than everyone had expected, which created an even more loving feeling throughout the house.

She'd longed for this all her life, to belong to a family, to be loved and to love in return. A small part of her felt sick about the fact that on Sunday she'd be returning to her lonely apartment in Los Angeles.

"There you are. Adam was wondering where you'd gone off to." Beverly Donovan entered the dining room coming up quietly behind Camille.

"Oh," she said, turning to face the matriarch of this family. "I just needed a moment alone."

Beverly wrapped her in a warm hug. "It's all right, dear. Losing your father was hard and then learning about all that treachery surrounding him had to be even harder. But it's over now. You're welcome here and I promise we'll do everything we can to make this the best Thanksgiving you've ever had."

Tears filled Camille's eyes and she dabbed at them before they could fall. "Thank you, Mrs. Donovan."

"Don't mention it. Now come along and get your seat right here next to me. Adam will sit on the other side of you."

Camille followed the woman and took her seat. The rest of the family filed in talking and taking their seats as well.

Adam kissed her briefly before sitting beside her.

Henry Donovan gave the blessing and the covered dishes on the table were opened. There was an abundance of food and a nice homey feel as Camille stacked her plate. Both Jade and Adam gave an approving nod as she did.

When everyone's plate was filled Adam tapped his fork to his glass and stood. "I'd like to make an announcement before everybody gets down to eating this wonderful feast."

Max groaned. "Why can't this announcement wait until after we've eaten this wonderful feast?"

Noelle nudged him. "I think he's serious."

"Thank you, Noelle." Adam nodded to her, then smiled down at Camille. "This is very important."

"A month or so ago Max and I thought we were venturing into another routine business deal. Then out of the blue a monkey wrench was thrown into that plan. A very beautiful and intelligent monkey wrench," he said gazing at Camille.

She blushed and fidgeted with her napkin.

"Up until that moment I'd sworn never to fall in love again. I never wanted to give another woman my heart or my soul. But I can't help it. Loving you is too easy," he said then pushed his chair back and got down on one knee.

Jade and Alma gasped. Linc and Henry smiled. And Beverly used her napkin to dab at her tears.

"With all my heart, my soul, my everlasting love I ask you, Camille Katherine Davis to be my wife."

Camille's heart pounded so loud she was certain

everyone else in the room could hear it. The napkin she'd been fidgeting with had fallen to the floor. Her eyes remained fixed on Adam's so that she wasn't totally aware when he pulled the little black box out of his jacket pocket and opened it in front of her.

But through her tears she spotted the glistening diamond and choked out a sob. "I...I don't know what to say."

"Say, yes, you'll marry me," Adam prompted and slipped the ring onto her finger.

Camille shook her head negatively and everybody looked at her as if she had just stolen something. "That just doesn't seem like enough," she said swiping her tears away with the back of her free hand.

"You didn't want to give your heart and soul. You didn't want to become seriously involved. But from the beginning it wasn't about any of that. Your concern was always for me. For my feelings, for my well-being, my happiness. For once in my life there was someone who was just concerned about me. That sounds so selfless and generous but then you showed that spoiled and dominant side."

There were snickers around the table and even Adam gave her a small smile. She touched her palm to his cheek and leaned closer.

"You demanded my heart and my soul. And I gave it to you, not because I felt guilty or because I didn't know any better, but because loving you was also easy."

She kissed his cheek.

"I love you so much, Adam. And nothing in this world could stop me from becoming your wife."

She kissed his lips.

Then as he was used to doing his hands found her hips and he lifted her out of the chair swinging her in the air as they kissed again.

Epilogue

"The house sold for eight and a half million dollars," Max announced on Christmas Eve as they sat in Linc's living room.

Camille clapped with glee. "That's double what we thought it would go for." She was sitting next to Adam who was smiling smugly.

"Good deal, Mr. Donovan," Adam said to Max and extended his hand for a shake.

"Great deal, Mr. Donovan." Max shook Adam's hand and smiled.

Camille cleared her throat.

Adam hugged her close. "Excellent deal, soon-to-be Mrs. Donovan."

She smiled. "Thank you."

Across the room a cell phone rang. Trent looked down on his hip and pulled it free. "Well, well, well," he said as he stood to leave the room. "I finally wore you down."

Jade came over to sit in the chair across from Adam and Camille. "What was that all about?"

Linc took a seat beside his wife. "You know Trent, it's probably one of his ladies."

Camille's lips spread into a huge smile. "It's a lady all right, but I don't know if Trent's ready for this one."

From boardroom to bedroom…

Brenda JACKSON

In Bed with Her Boss

Though D'marcus Armstrong is a demanding, cranky boss, he's the star of Opal Lockhart's fantasies. But what chance does a buttoned-up, naive secretary have with this self-made millionaire? A pretty good one actually…when Opal's sisters come to the rescue with a makeover and some attitude adjustment!

THE LOCKHARTS
THREE WEDDINGS & A REUNION

*Available the first week of August
wherever books are sold.*

KIMANI™
ROMANCE

Good girl behaving badly!

J.M. JEFFRIES

VIRGIN SEDUCTRESS

Nell Evans's plans for a new life don't include
being a virgin at 30. And with the help of bad
boy Riley Martin, that's about to change. Riley
can't believe an offer of seduction coming from
the sweet, shy woman of his secret fantasies—
but he's determined to convince her that her
place is with him…forever.

*Available the first week of August
wherever books are sold.*

**KIMANI™
ROMANCE**

www.kimanipress.com   KPJMJ0300807

Essence bestselling author

PATRICIA HALEY

Still Waters

A poignant and memorable story about a once-loving
husband who has lost his way...and his spiritual wife
who has grown weary from constantly praying for
the marriage. Greg and Laurie Wright are perched at
the edge of an all-out crisis—and only a miracle can
restore what's been lost.

"Patricia Haley has written a unique work of
Christian fiction that should not be missed."
—*Rawsistaz Reviewers* on *No Regrets*

*Available the first week of August
wherever books are sold.*

NEW SPIRIT
TM

www.kimanipress.com   KPPH0730807

Celebrating life every step of the way.

YOU ONLY GET *Better*

New York Times bestselling author

CONNIE BRISCOE

and

Essence bestselling authors

LOLITA FILES
ANITA BUNKLEY

Three fortysomething women discover that life, men and
everything else get better with age in this entertaining
three-in-one anthology from three award-winning authors!

Available the first week of March wherever books are sold.

KIMANI PRESS™
www.kimanipress.com

KPYOGB0590307